Tying the Noose

Felicity Philips Investigates

Book 2

Steve Higgs

Text Copyright © 2021 Steven J Higgs

Publisher: Steve Higgs

The right of Steve Higgs to be identified as author of the Work has been asserted by him in accordance with the Copyright, Designs and Patents Act 1988

All rights reserved.

The book is copyright material and must not be copied, reproduced, transferred, distributed, leased, licensed or publicly performed or used in any way except as specifically permitted in writing by the publishers, as allowed under the terms and conditions under which it was purchased or as strictly permitted by applicable copyright law. Any unauthorised distribution or use of this text may be a direct infringement of the author's and publisher's rights and those responsible may be liable in law accordingly.

'Tying the Noose' is a work of fiction. Names, characters, businesses, organisations, places, events and incidents either are the product of the author's imagination or are used fictitiously. Any resemblance to actual persons, living or dead, events or locations is entirely coincidental.

Dedication

While writing this book, my precious daughter, the only one I have, turned one. I waited a long time before deciding I wanted children. Too long almost.

Hermione Rose Higgs is at that age where every day brings something new. Be it a new word, a new skill, or a new behaviour, my decision to quit working for other people and attempt a career as an author enables me to be with her to witness these things.

With her hair in bunches and a beaming smile on her face, she looks like a cartoonist's impression of a baby girl.

I love you, Hermione.

Table of Contents

- The Storm
- Suicide
- Hate Crime
- Murder?
- Cats, Dogs, and Secret Passages
- Volunteered
- A Terrible Sleuth
- Rising Body Count
- Thinking Like a Detective
- Someone in the Dark
- Room to Room
- Unexpected Late Arrival
- Humans are Boring
- Mindy
- Discoveries
- Guilty
- Faint
- Utter Confusion and Horror
- Dominant Male
- Cats
- Destruction
- Accomplice
- In the Clouds
- Low Point
- Devil Dog Time
- Massive Incongruity

Returning Resolve

Shameful Guilt

Confronting a Killer

The Big Reveal

Chase in the Dark

Mopping Up

Epilogue: The Call

Author's Note

What's next for Felicity Philips?

A FREE Rex and Albert Story

More Cozy Mystery by Steve Higgs

Free Books and More

The Storm

The sky outside looked angry. It was as if it had been suffering outrages for weeks and was now full to its stomach with unquenchable rage.

My window overlooked the causeway which linked Raven Island to the English mainland and my home county of Kent. Waves were starting to crash over it as the storm built, forcing me to question how many times in the past the road might have been washed away by nature's irrepressible energy.

My name is Felicity Philips. I'm a wedding planner who specialises in the very high end, celebrity and ultra-rich end of the market. The wedding this weekend was completely typical for me in that it had a seven-figure price tag, a guest list with pop stars and TV personalities, and was the result of many months of planning.

The groom and groom, a celebrity couple with faces many in the country would recognise, were tying the knot in a private function – hence the island retreat – among hundreds of friends and relatives. It often amazed me just how many people could come out of the woodwork for a celebrity wedding. Surely no one actually considered three hundred people to be their close personal friends?

The number of guests wasn't a problem; the more the merrier for me since I was charging per head for many of the wedding's elements.

It was set to be a fun weekend, and yes, there would be times when I was rushed off my feet trying to make sure everything was done, but equally, as the person in charge, I ran things in such a way that I delegated most of the work to others.

One of those who took a load off my back was my master of ceremonies, Justin Metcalf. He was one of those people who stayed calm no matter what might be going on around him. He was due to arrive tomorrow morning when the tide would once again expose the causeway, and just in time for the weekend of festivities to begin.

I was here a day early to get settled in and begin receiving people. The grooms were also here along with some of their closest friends to enjoy a relaxed evening together before the ceremony. Also on the island was a pair of chefs, some florists, who were sprucing the place up with many thousands of pounds worth of fresh blooms, and the wedding photographer, Quentin Falstaff, a man I'd worked with for years and considered to be a good friend.

'It's really picking up out there, Auntie,' commented Mindy, my assistant and niece. She was staying in a room which adjoined mine. The great house we were in wasn't a hotel, it was a private residence which made it different from most weddings in that very few of the guests could be accommodated at the venue. Everyone else was staying in hotels on the mainland.

I took Mindy on a few months ago, which is to say my elder sister bullied me into it. It was proving to be a smart move though, for although at nineteen Mindy was like most teenagers and easily distracted, she had other characteristics which had recently made her a valuable asset.

I was about to agree with her when I spotted what she was wearing. I cocked an eyebrow.

'Mindy, please tell me you are about to get changed.'

Mindy looked at what I was wearing. I had a blue and green dress that did a great job of making me look taller than the five feet and five inches I managed to achieve. Mindy towered over me and would happily wear huge heels to make her over six feet tall as she strutted around. I wore more conservative heels these days. Well into my fifties, I am not a fan of sore feet. In contrast to the outfit I wore, which was perfect wedding planner attire, Mindy chose to clad herself in outdoor, rugged sportswear.

She was naturally athletic and moved with a sinuous grace; her choice of clothes allowed her to move fast if she needed to, but training as my understudy, she needed to look, act, and speak the same way I did.

'I'll get changed shortly, Auntie,' she promised.

I was about to give her specific instructions on which items to wear when, from the corner of my eye, I saw a set of headlights coming across the causeway. 'There's someone out there!' I gasped, barely able to believe my eyes. 'They're going to get washed away!'

Mindy rushed to my side at the window. 'Oh, wow,' she murmured when another giant wave hit the edge of the road and the car was lost to sight.

For a second, it looked as if the wave had taken the car, dragging it and whoever might be inside back into the roiling sea. It would spell certain death if that were the case, but we both relaxed and took a breath when the headlights appeared again.

Her voice a soft murmur, Mindy said, 'Whoever that is sure wants to get to this island. I thought they closed the causeway already?'

'They did,' I murmured, wondering who could be so reckless as to charge through the storm and risk their life just to get here.

Mindy frowned, 'Who else is coming today?'

I didn't know the answer to that question. Most of the wedding guests who were staying in the house, a palatial folly called Raven's Bluff, had arrived an hour ago, getting across the causeway the moment it opened.

The tide only dropped far enough to expose it twice a day and for about a two hour stretch each time. The arrival of the storm changed that, lifting the tide prematurely while also making it far more treacherous. No one had attempted to cross it in the last thirty minutes and there was no one from my end of things due to arrive until tomorrow.

The florists were supposed to be returning to the mainland before the causeway shut but it was clear the storm would trap them here. I doubted that would be too much of a problem. They would be found accommodation and given both food and drinks this evening. They could escape in the morning and would have something to talk about in their shop on Monday.

Squinting into the murk outside, I tracked the car's progress. The outline and colour were beginning to take shape – it was still light out despite the gloom the storm had brought. There was something familiar about the car, something … unsettling. I couldn't place why I felt that way but just as a ball of doubt began to form in my gut, a scream ripped through the air.

The suddenness of it made me jump and caused Buster, my Bulldog, to bark his surprise.

'*Cor, what was that?*' he asked, rolling to get his paws beneath his body. He'd been asleep on his back for the last half an hour, snoring like an industrial sawmill.

My cat, Amber, was asleep too, but all the reaction we got from her was a solitary eye opening. She closed it again having decided a human in peril somewhere nearby really wasn't a good enough reason to be awake.

Mindy was reaching behind her back with her right arm, feeling for what she probably had hidden in the small of her back.

I shook my head at her, and she dropped her hand back to her side as we ran for the door. My niece is part ninja having eschewed gymnastics classes for martial arts training instead. Her father took her in secret for more than a decade, both knowing Mindy's mother would not approve. Now she had a worrying habit for keeping a blunt weapon about her person.

I call it a worrying habit, yet it had already proved useful more than once in the last week or so.

I was on my way to the hallway outside, wanting to know what might have caused the horrified shriek. Mindy joined me, so too Buster, scurrying along at my feet as fast as his stumpy legs would carry him.

'*I bet it's another body*,' puffed Buster with excitement.

The possibility that we were rushing to find that someone had been murdered had not occurred to me until that point, but at Buster's words, my head filled with images from the last couple of weeks.

Ever since the wedding at Loxton Hall, my life had been one long, strange, and unwelcome adventure.

Bursting through my door and into the hallway outside, I tried to pinpoint where the scream might have come from and thus which way we needed to go. The sound of running feet came from our left, out of sight around the corner somewhere. Others were on their way to see who had screamed and why.

My niece and dog shot off as I remained stationary outside the door to my room, and I might have decided to go back inside had one of the grooms, Geoffrey Banks, not appeared in the hallway. He was coming from the other direction, a worried expression dominating his features, and he was not alone. More people appeared, all hustling to see what drama might be unfolding. I knew I had no choice but to go with them – it's my job to make sure the weekend runs smoothly.

Having memorised the guestlist and making a point of learning everyone's names, I spotted Irina Kalashnikov, a TV show host for a glitzy reality show, Laughing Boy, AKA Matt Finn, who was a radio show host and known for having a droll voice, and Gazelle Hubbard, a former glamour model turned actress who was in the same soap opera as Geoffrey.

At an intersecting hallway, we all met and turned to go down it.

Geoffrey was running faster than his generous frame suggested he did very often.

He shouted, 'That was Anton!' as he puffed and panted along the hallway.

The news quickened my feet – the other groom was in trouble!

Buster was snorting and grunting, breathing heavily through his poorly shaped nose as he tried to keep up. He was also getting in the way, his blocky body taking up a lot of floor space and he had no thought for other people. He ran in a straight line, barging through gaps that were not there if he needed to.

I found myself constantly apologising. 'Sorry. Sorry about the dog. Buster! Watch where you are going. Sorry!'

Reaching the next corner, he didn't slow down, he just flopped onto his belly and slid across the carpet, digging a back paw in to create a turn. At the same time, he yelled, *'Power slide!'* with more exuberance and excitement than the situation called for.

Incredibly, his daft belly flop/slide proved to be the swiftest way for him to change direction and he came out of it running again but now facing the right way.

A couple of staff from the stately home were in the corridor ahead of us when we turned a corner. They were slow-moving, both in their seventies or eighties and going the wrong way. The house didn't have many staff, that much I discovered in my first visit many months ago when I was taken on for the job.

The house only had one occupant - a famous author called Boris Benton, and thus he managed quite adequately with almost no people to help him.

'This way,' I frowned at them as they tucked in to let us by. 'You must have heard that guest shouting.'

The man muttered something I didn't catch, but when I glanced over my shoulder, they were both following.

We were nearing the front of the house where it looks toward the Kent coast and the causeway that links one to the other, when a man stepped into the hallway ahead of us. He was coming out of the honeymoon suite, our obvious destination since Geoffrey said it was his intended's voice he heard.

It was the other groom, Anton Harker. A daytime TV presenter and household name, Anton Harker was a larger-than-life character with a beaming smile. A favourite with many demographics, the man in his late forties was known for his permatan and incredible hair. But right now, the mischievous twinkle that made him famous was gone from his eyes. His face was so white I thought I might be able to see through it if he turned sideways. He clung to the doorframe like it was the only thing keeping him up and it was then that I noticed he was wearing nothing but a bathrobe.

Geoffrey's hand shot to his mouth. 'Anton, what is it, darling?'

Momentarily discombobulated by events, I wanted to know what the heck Anton might have seen to affect him so severely.

I found out soon enough.

Suicide

The central focus of the room was a fourposter bed. It was a grand looking thing with ornately carved posts rising from the floor to a height of about seven feet. Curtains hung so they could be drawn around it to ward out the cold though I doubted they were ever used for such a purpose any longer.

It was a feature that suited the large room Boris, the owner, had designated as the one best suited for the honeymooners. The bed, however, was not the thing that drew the eye, it was the man hanging by his neck from a rope just a few yards to its left.

I took a sharp intake of breath, gasping like a fish stuck on the shore.

'This room smells of cat,' complained Buster, plonking his back end on the carpet with an audible thump.

The man was hanging away from us so we could not see the face. I didn't need to though; I knew who it was.

Coming to my senses, I yelled, 'Quick! Get him down!'

Jarred into motion by my words, Mindy, Geoffrey, and others all ran at the dangling form.

A rope had been looped over an exposed wooden beam, of which there were several in the room, left there deliberately for their aesthetic appearance no doubt. It was tied to a hook next to one of the large windows, there to keep the curtains in place. The hook was bending under the weight of the form hanging from the noose.

Mindy uttered a few colourful words when she saw who it was.

She had been closest to the window and got the rope free just as Geoffrey and Matt Finn took the hanged man's weight. The men lowered him to the carpet and as they did so, something tumbled free of his jacket.

Mindy, being closest, crouched to look at it. 'It's a note,' she remarked needlessly; it was obvious to us all what it was.

As they got Quentin to the floor, I stepped in – I needed to know if he was still alive or not. Doing my best to ignore the terrible look on his face, I touched my fingers to his neck.

'There's no pulse,' I whimpered.

'His neck is snapped,' said Matt Finn. 'Who is he?'

'It's Quentin Falstaff,' I murmured, my brain barely able to comprehend what I was seeing as I stared down into the man's lifeless eyes.

'*Really?*' said Buster. '*It doesn't smell like him.*'

Mindy was still crouching over the slip of paper on the floor. It looked to be a sheet torn from a notepad, the type that has the curly-whirly ring thing going along the top. It was face down.

Curling her lip, Mindy extended one manicured fingernail and flipped it over. She had to crane her head a little to read it as it wasn't facing her.

'I'm sorry. I can't take anymore,' she read.

I got back to upright and stumbled across to Mindy so I could read it for myself. It made no sense. He was happily chatting with me half an hour ago.

All around me were other people – more than a dozen of them – all of whom had heard Anton's fearful wail and come running.

Quentin was staring into nothing, his eyes locked open as rigour began to set in. I wanted to close them, but also didn't want to touch him.

Matt Finn stood up too, stepping back away from the body just as everyone else already had. Geoffrey was with Anton, giving him comfort.

'You knew him, Mrs Philips?' I turned to see who had spoken, finding the house manager standing behind me.

It was someone I knew by name. 'Yes, Ellis. He and I have worked together for many years. He has a wife and four children.' I only just got the last few words out. I didn't really know his wife and children; I thought of Quentin as a friend, but we didn't mix much other than at work. Nevertheless, that his children were now fatherless was a terrible blow I found myself reeling from.

Ellis Carter was taking charge, holding his arms out to his sides as yet more people arrived at the doorway to the honeymoon suite. He was an average looking man, by which I mean he had a face that would not stick in one's memory, but at the same time, it was perfectly pleasant to look at.

I guessed his height at a shade under six feet, which made him neither tall nor short and his age at just the right side of forty. His hair was a dull brown shade and cut short so it matched the stubble on his face. His eyes were brown and a little watery and he had no ring on his finger to indicate he had a life beyond the management of Raven's Bluff.

'I think we should all exit the room and leave it as preserved as possible for the police and the coroner,' he said while taking a sheet from the bed. He used it to cover the body lying face up on the carpet on the left side of the bed.

'But this is our honeymoon suite,' protested Geoffrey.

My eyes flared slightly but this was where I needed to step in as the wedding planner. The events I organise never run smoothly and it is the job of my team to ensure the bridal party (not sure that term works this time) never became aware of the effort going on behind the scenes.

That wasn't going to be so easy this time since the grooms were already aware they had a body in their bedroom, but I was going to do my best anyway.

'We will have all your things shifted to a new suite,' I promised. 'There are many suites here almost as plush as this one.' I could see Geoffrey was about to protest, so quickly added, 'It's not like we can move the body.'

I was operating largely on autopilot with Mindy holding my arm for support. How on earth was Quentin dead? I was talking to him just a short while ago. He gave no indication that he wanted to take his own life. Given the timeframe, he must have finished talking to me, and come directly to the honeymoon suite to hang himself.

I couldn't make sense of it.

When no one moved, Ellis Carter said, 'Please. Everyone. I must insist.'

'Ha!' huffed a voice from over by the door. The people there spread out slightly as they turned to see who made the noise. 'There'll be no police, and no coroner to take the body away any time soon,' cackled an old man in Raven's Bluff livery. He was one of the pair I passed in the hallway. 'That's an Easterly blowing out there. At least a force nine or ten.

No one's getting anywhere near this island until the storm blows itself out or moves away.'

'What do you mean, Eric?' asked Mr Carter.

Eric moved into the middle of the room so he was equidistance from the door and the foot of the bed. Once there, he pirouetted slowly on the spot, taking in as many eyes as possible.

'You young'uns and visitors have no knowledge of this island, so let me tell you,' his voice was croaky and rough. It gave his words a creepy edge as if he were predicting our collective doom. 'The causeway is closed. They'll have shut it off at the mainland end by now anyway, but even if the rising tide didn't make it impassable, the storm surely will. No boats will be able to cross either, so we're stuck here until the storm's energy dissipates.'

As if on cue, a flash lit the room and a thunderbolt cracked overhead before my heart could beat again.

Irina Kalashnikov squealed in fright which made half the people in the room jump. She laughed nervously at herself, fanning her face with both hands.

We were trapped here by the sea and the storm, but it wasn't just us. I'd spoken to Quentin not less than thirty minutes ago and that had to mean …

'I dare say you've brought it on yourselves,' said a new voice, this time a woman.

'Ah, that's enough of that, thank you, Hattie,' insisted Ellis in his best manager's voice. 'Eric, I think you had better take your wife away.'

'I'll do no such thing,' snapped Eric.

I looked at the Raven's Bluff staff, a standoff occurring right before not only my eyes but also those of the wedding guests and both of my grooms.

'What is going on?' I wanted to know. We were all still crowded around the body, twenty or more people either in the suite or peering curiously through the door from outside. We needed to get out and close the door. If the police couldn't come for many hours, then so be it, but having a row a few feet from Quentin's body was unseemly.

'Not another word,' warned Ellis, his eyes narrowed at both Eric and Hattie.

'It's unnatural,' spat Hattie, her eyes filled with hate as she glared at the grooms. Like a punch to the gut, I understood what this was.

'Mr Carter, I must insist you clear the room of your staff. I will not tolerate this. I will speak with you and your staff separately in my suite.'

His face flushed from embarrassment over the old couple's behaviour, Ellis put his arms out to guide Eric back toward the door.

Hattie wasn't done though. 'It's disgusting!' she spat from her evil mouth.

Geoffrey suddenly cottoned on. 'Is this about us?'

'Aye,' added Eric. 'Unholy and ungodly. It ought not be allowed. Your kind should all be flogged,' the old man growled as he ambled toward the door.

Homophobia at its worst and displayed the night before their wedding in their honeymoon suite. I was mortified.

The old couple was ushered from the room, all eyes turned their way though the disbelieving and horrified stares they received seemed to not register at all.

'I am so sorry,' I blushed as I approached the grooms. We were all leaving the room now, the people at the door stepping back to give us space. 'I have never seen such a terrible display. Please be assured I had no idea that could even happen. I will be addressing this issue with the house management immediately. There will be no further such occurrences if I have anything to do with it.'

Geoffrey and Anton looked stunned. First a murder in their bedroom, then a shameful homophobic attack. Anton was getting some of his colour back but clung to his lover for support. We were in the hallway outside their room. Wedding guests were milling around, some drifting away, others hanging around as if they had a question to ask or wanted another look at Quentin's body.

Ellis and Mindy were the last two to leave the honeymoon suite, Mr Carter closing the door and locking it as he joined us in the hallway.

I steeled myself for the verbal assault I expected from the grooms, but mercifully, none came. Instead, the couple was understanding and kind.

'Felicity, none of this is your doing,' sighed Geoffrey.

'Yes,' agreed Anton. 'Listen to us complaining about our room. He was a friend of yours?'

I hung my head, the heartrending knowledge that Quentin was dead still sinking in and hard to believe. I gave them a nod, unsure what my voice might do if I were to try to speak.

'You poor dear,' said Geoffrey, letting go of Anton so he could wrap me in a hug. Anton came too, both men sandwiching me almost as they put their arms around me.

'Perhaps a stiff drink is in order,' suggested Anton. 'We brought a lovely forty-year-old scotch ...' his voice tailed off. 'I just remembered. It's in our bedroom.'

'I'm fine,' I lied. 'You are my priority, gentlemen. This is your weekend, your event. I would have nothing interrupt it for you. Obviously, I cannot undo what has been done,' I sighed and shuddered, my body responding badly to my need to weep. 'I will arrange to have your things moved as soon as I can. If you could please allow me long enough to make arrangements with Boris and Mr Carter ...'

'Of course,' replied Anton. 'I, um ... I could do with some clothes.'

The poor man was still in his bathrobe and most likely getting a little cool since he was still damp.

We were standing outside the door to their suite. Obviously, the couple needed to go back inside to collect a few of their things and I wasn't going to stop them. I had no reason to and no authority even if I thought it necessary.

'*Someone's coming*,' said Buster, his comment unheard by anyone but me.

Ellis unlocked the door once more so the grooms could get what they needed. They did their best to not look at the sad form beneath the sheet to their left and held each other for mutual support.

I watched them, hanging around to give them my support because working gave me something to focus on – and I needed that.

Waiting for Anton and Geoffrey to reappear, I heard footsteps coming our way.

Hate Crime

Hurrying toward me was the current owner of Raven's Bluff. An eccentric writer whose books propelled him to international stardom. Then a Hollywood movie deal took him from just ordinary rich to superrich. However, Boris Benton was a man who mostly wanted to be left alone. Why else would a person buy a house that could only be reached twice a day?

He was in his late fifties and single, having lost his wife to cancer quite publicly at exactly the same time he became a household name. At five feet and six inches, he was on the short side but didn't stoop to wearing Cuban heels or orthotics to make himself taller. His hair was grey and fading to white, but he had a full head of it above steely blue eyes and a kind, if sad, smile.

Stardom brought him money, but with it the loss of privacy. He was a long-time friend to Geoffrey, who only announced himself as gay less than a year ago. As a wedding gift, Boris opened his house so the celebrity grooms might also enjoy the seclusion it offered for their special day.

'Mr Benton,' I sighed sorrowfully as he approached. I knew he was allowing this event as a wedding gift to his friend but a murder on the premises would bring the police and then reporters, the very things he didn't want. 'I'm so sorry this has happened.'

'Did you help him to kill himself?' Boris asked, still hurrying along the corridor toward me.

The question hit me like a slap to the face. 'Of course not, how …'

Boris held up a hand to quieten me. 'Then you cannot be blamed for what has happened and should feel no need to apologise for it, Mrs

Philips.' He offered me kind eyes and took both my hands in his. 'Ellis tells me the, um … dead man is … was a friend of yours.'

I sniffed as a tear escaped my left eye and the emotions bubbling away behind my façade came to the surface.

I managed to just about blub, 'He was such a nice man!' but it came out as a wail of despair.

Mindy came to me, putting an arm around my shoulders and Buster nudged up against my leg, offering his presence as comfort.

Boris took over, opening the door just a crack to speak with Geoffrey and Anton inside and he directed Ellis to help me get back to my room. A stiff drink was beginning to sound quite appealing, that and a lie down, but even as I allowed the young man to guide me along the hallways, the voice inside my head was arguing that there was too much to do.

The voice won, my feet digging into the carpet as I wiped my eyes and told myself off. I was THE wedding planner, the best in the county, if not the country and weeping women do not get appointed to plan the next royal wedding.

That was my ultimate aim, so I was going to be strong and would do what was right.

'Auntie, where are you going?' asked Mindy when I slipped from her grip and reversed direction.

'There is work to do, Mindy. I will cry for Quentin later.' I was still crying now, truth be told, but I was going to wrestle that under control.

Boris was still standing at the door to the honeymoon suite, conversing with Geoffrey and Anton through the gap in the door as they quickly packed enough bits to survive for a few hours. He saw me coming, surprise registering on his face.

'Is there something wrong, Felicity?' he asked.

I shook my head. 'There is a lot wrong, Boris. A lot. However, my focus must be on the grooms. They are what matters. We need to get these gentlemen moved to another room, Mr Benton. I would attend to this myself, but the bulk of my staff will not arrive until tomorrow. I need to borrow a couple of your staff.'

He pulled an 'oops' face. 'But I only operate a skeleton staff, Felicity. That's why you had a cleaning crew in this week to refresh the house. I have five members of staff and two of them are about to be sacked. Besides Ellis here, I have a cook and a gardener and they both have the weekend off because you have brought your own people.'

I sniffed in a deep breath. 'Right. Not to worry. Please leave it with me.' Basically, the task was going to fall to Mindy and me. I couldn't see another way around it. 'I just need a room to which we can move them.'

Boris consulted the inside of his head for a moment, but before he could provide an answer, my niece posed a question that derailed any plans we might have been about to make.

'Where's his camera?'

Murder?

Buster instantly started sniffing and snuffling around the carpet as he sampled different smells and began listing them.

It was true that Quentin never went anywhere without his camera. On the occasions when he and I had shared dinner or a drink – usually when we were away somewhere for a wedding as we were this time – he would still have at least one hung around his neck.

While I was ignoring the obvious body under the sheet, Mindy had been examining it and noticed the discrepancy.

'It's probably in his room,' I replied, my mind on other things.

Buster turned around to look at me. '*Why was he even in here?*'

Mindy shot me a look. 'What did he say?'

Her question in turn caused the four men in the room to all give me quizzical looks. If you are wondering what that is all about, it's quite simple. I can hear what my dog says. His thoughts and words arrive in my head as fully formed sentences though everyone else just hears him bark, whine, or growl. The same is true for my cat, Amber.

It is only those two animals – the two I live with. I had this as a child until my parents got fed up with their *strange* daughter and gave our pets away. It only reoccurred when, after my husband died, I chose to visit an animal rehoming centre and picked out the two animals I now find myself having conversations with.

Mindy caught me talking to Buster a while ago and she knows my secret. Unfortunately, she isn't bright enough to keep it a secret.

'You can understand the dog?' asked Geoffrey.

I snorted a small laugh. 'Of course not.' Then, flaring my eyes at Mindy while she had the decency to blush at her indiscretion, I asked, 'Any idea why Quentin was in your suite?'

My question was posed toward the two grooms. Anton turned inward to look at Geoffrey who blushed crimson.

'I bumped into him twenty minutes ago. He said something about meeting in our suite as arranged. I didn't know what he was talking about, but it was obvious he was the photographer, so I figured he just meant he wanted to talk to us about our preferences for pictures and where we might want to have them taken.'

That sounded just like something Quentin would do. Geoffrey was about to say something else when a question formed in my head.

'Did he have a rope with him?'

My words hung in the air as everyone turned to look at Geoffrey.

Put on the spot, the TV star had a panicked look but was confident when he said, 'No. If there had been a rope, I don't see how I could have missed it. He had his camera in both hands.'

'The camera that is now missing,' Mindy reminded us. 'Auntie …'

'Don't say it,' I warned her.

'*Felicity*,' whined Buster, looking up at me from under the bed still.

'How else can we explain it?' Mindy pestered.

'What's going on?' asked Boris. Like the other men, he was confused and bemused by the conversation I was having with my niece.

I sighed and let my shoulders drop in defeat. I didn't want to admit it. Heck, I didn't even want to think about it, but the clues were screaming in my face.

I took a deep breath, wondering what I might have done to deserve the position I now found myself in, but lifted my eyes to meet those of the grooms' and the owner of the house.

'Mindy is suggesting that Quentin Falstaff didn't hang himself.' I got further confused looks in return. So I did my best to clarify what I was telling them. 'He was murdered.'

My statement stilled everyone; all eyes widened as they considered the possibility that the man beneath the sheet might not have taken his own life.

The tension in the room was so thick it felt like it ought to be visible, so when a cat screeched a wild shriek of displeasure from under the bed, I was not the only one who almost wet themselves.

Buster shot out from under the valance, making it billow with his passage like the hem of a skirt in the wind. Clearly the cat had startled him too because he was yelping like a terrified puppy.

'*Arrrrgh!*' He shot between my legs, almost knocking me over in the process. '*I said it smelled of cat!*'

Mindy dropped to the floor, falling into a press up position to look under the four-poster. She was on the opposite side, over near Quentin's body and thus vanished from view.

When her head popped up again a moment later, she asked, 'Did it come out that side?'

My eyebrows waggled in question. 'No. No sign of it here.'

'Well, I didn't imagine it,' coughed Buster. *'Big as a bear it was. Huge. Big pointy teeth and claws the size of the Devil's scythe.'* I eyed him sceptically. *'And it had an eyepatch*,' he added.

Now I knew he was making it up.

'Don't worry, Buster. I won't tell Amber the little kitty scared you.'

'There's nothing under the bed,' Mindy assured us all as she bounced nimbly back to her feet.

I was about to ask her how sure she was – I hadn't imagined the cat squawking – when Boris offered an explanation.

'There are cats living in the house. I couldn't tell you how many, only that they were here when I moved in and they live in the walls. There are gaps, you see?' he explained. 'This is a folly, built for design, not purpose, and thus more than a little odd. The original owner was a cat lover, and the ones here now are most likely direct descendants of those first cats. There are gaps between the walls so they can move about. There are no plans for the house, so I have no idea where they connect. What I do know is that they are too small for a human to fit but allow cats to move freely around the house.'

Mindy gasped, 'Coooool!'

Buster harrumphed, *'Great. There are evil cats in the walls who can attack from any angle even if all the doors are locked.'*

I put the subject to one side. 'We need to get everyone together and make sure we are all accounted for. There is a team of florists here, your staff,' I nodded my head at Boris, 'a few wedding guests. There was a delivery driver from my caterer here earlier and two members of the kitchen staff were sent in advance to receive the food.'

Geoffrey added, 'There are a few of our friends looking for accommodation over on the mainland. They got cut off by the storm.' Most of the wedding guests were set to join Anton and Geoffrey tomorrow but it did not surprise me to hear some who were due to arrive today didn't get to the causeway in time.

I nodded, unhappy that I was somehow in charge of this mess. I came here to manage a wedding, not deal with a possible murder, but the form under the sheet just a few feet away demanded at least some investigation, if only so we could prove one way or another if there was …

The shocking thought taking shape in my mind was interrupted by Ellis asking me a question.

'Should your dog be doing that?' asked Ellis, clearly meaning that whatever Buster was doing he ought to not be.

I turned to find my Bulldog sniffing Quentin.

'Buster,' I hissed insistently.

'*Just getting his scent*,' Buster replied without turning his head or moving away.

'Buster, come away,' I hissed again with even more urgency in my voice. In truth, I was fine with him getting Quentin's scent. He could use his nose to find out things no human investigator could, but now, with people watching him, was not the right time.

Buster took a final snuffle of air before turning to his left and trotting back to me.

'*There is another smell on him. Another person*,' Buster told me.

I couldn't answer, so I crouched to pat his head, and said, 'Good boy.'

'*I'll be able to identify them if I smell them again,*' he assured me.

Coming out of the crouch, the shocking thought returned, making me gasp audibly.

'What is it, Auntie?' asked Mindy, seeing me freeze to the spot.

With my pulse banging in my head and my breaths coming fast, I turned to meet her. 'I spoke with Quentin less than half an hour before we found his body.'

'Okay?' she replied, not sure what I was trying to say.

Geoffrey got it though.

'The storm shut off the causeway before that,' he murmured, the colour draining from his face.

Anton said, 'So? So what?'

Swivelling around to face the grooms, I said, 'We are trapped here. If Quentin was murdered …'

'Then the killer is trapped here too!' blurted Boris.

Cats, Dogs, and Secret Passages

Half an hour later, I was in my room and looking out the window once more. The causeway was now nowhere in sight, the tide had swallowed it to leave no trace that it had ever been there. We were just more than a mile from the mainland, but with the storm raging outside, we might as well have been in the middle of the Atlantic.

I had a crystal tumbler in my right hand, the contents of which were all but gone. Only the dregs remained, and I tossed them back as I pushed away from the view outside.

Elsewhere, Boris and Ellis were doing their best to round up everyone in the house. You might think they ought to be rounding up everyone on the island, but Raven's Bluff is the only inhabited structure on the outcropping of jagged rock. We needed to get them together to break the news. That was the excuse we were using at least. There was more to it though.

When we left the honeymoon suite, we went directly to Quentin's room. I wanted to confirm my awful suspicions but Boris, Geoffrey, Anton, and Ellis Carter, the house manager, all came too, keen to know what we were up against.

Quentin's camera wasn't there either, and alarmingly, neither was his laptop. More damningly, the handwriting on the suicide note, which Mindy snapped a picture of using her phone before we left the honeymoon suite, did not match. We found a small diary in which Quentin kept his appointments. It seems like an odd thing to do in the twenty-first century – Mindy marvelled at it like a person might if shown a time machine.

The notebook from which the page had been torn was not found in his room. Its absence was hardly conclusive evidence but when added to the pile of clues already staring us in the face no one argued with my belief that my friend was a victim of foul play.

Ellis had called the police after we searched Quentin's room. Someone had to do it and he volunteered. He got to speak to a detective sergeant called Khan who, according to Ellis, took his claim that the obvious suicide was suspicious at face value. At least he didn't dismiss it.

DS Khan wasn't coming to look for himself though; the storm dictated that no one would, just as creepy old Eric predicted. He asked us to stay calm, leave the body where it was and to make sure no one messed with it. He would have a team across to us as soon as the weather permitted.

Rain hammered against the window. It was raining cats and dogs. As that familiar phrase popped into my head, I turned to look at Buster. I had just remembered something.

'You said it didn't smell like Quentin,' I reminded my Bulldog.

He was lying flat on the carpet, his jaw flush with it which always made him look like one of those old bearskin rugs. His jowls flopped over his bottom teeth to leave his canines poking upward like tusks.

'*S'right*,' he mumbled.

'*You're not trusting the dog's sense of smell, are you?*' enquired Amber. My Ragdoll cat was still on the bed, curled up with her front paws tucked under her body. She looked to be asleep but clearly wasn't. '*I'm surprised the dog can ever smell anything other than his own farts.*'

Buster was instantly on his paws and scrambling at the side of the bed as he tried to climb it. Knowing he couldn't scale it to get to her, Amber didn't bother to move.

'Calm down, Buster,' I soothed.

Amber rolled onto her back in a display of nonchalance – the dog barking a few inches from her head didn't bother her at all.

'All I'm saying,' she purred, *'Is that his nose isn't reliable. I can take a sniff if you like.'*

'What!' snarled Buster. *'Dogs do the smelling,'*

'They certainly do,' agreed Amber cruelly.

'Arrrgh. That's not what I meant, and you know it, cat. Dogs have the most powerful noses. Cats only use theirs as something to look down.'

He had a point there.

The comment rolled off Amber as she sniggered. *'Oh, dear, Buster. I wouldn't have to look down my nose at you, if dogs were not so far beneath me.'*

My pets could argue like this for hours, trading insults needlessly and fruitlessly simply because they were different species, and each viewed the other as inferior.

I interrupted. 'Buster, if it didn't smell like Quentin, what did it smell of?'

Whatever fresh insult he had lined up for the cat died on his lips and he turned his attention my way.

'When I came into the room, the first scent I got was the stench of cat.' I remembered he made a comment at the time to that effect. 'There was another scent behind it though. I only got Quentin's particular odour when I got close to him and then I could smell him and there was the scent of another man on Quentin's clothing.'

'The scent of his killer?'

Buster tilted his head and looked up at me. 'I can't tell that from the smell. I just know Quentin's clothing smelled of someone else. The additional scent would have got there through physical contact.'

It was good enough to convince me. Buster had picked up the scent of Quentin's killer and would be able to identify him again.

'So what was the other scent in the room? If you could smell cat, and Quentin and the other man's scent on Quentin's clothing, what was the other smell you found?'

'A woman,' Buster stated not sounding entirely sure of himself.

'You see,' sighed Amber, lazily rolling on her back.

'Ignore her, Buster,' I begged, before he could react. 'Tell me what you could smell.'

'It was definitely a woman, but she wasn't in season.' I rolled my eyes, certain that was detail I had no use for. 'Her scent was faint,' he explained. 'I could smell that stuff you put under your arms, plus perfume. It was floral, but not one that you wear.'

That didn't do much to narrow it down.

'Would you recognise it if you smelled it again?' I asked him.

I got a tail wag. 'Absolutely.'

'*Bravo,*' commented Amber sarcastically.

Buster growled at her, '*The stench of cat in the room wasn't helping.*'

His reply reminded me that I wanted to ask Amber a question.

'Amber there are cats in this house. One of them was under the bed in the room where Quentin died.'

Amber rolled onto her paws and sat up, lifting her front right paw to inspect it. '*Yes, I met some of them.*'

'So what I wanted to know was … hold on. When did you meet them?'

Amber flicked her eyes up to meet mine. '*When you went out. You ran from the room and the cats came to investigate. They don't often get new cats in here and they were curious. Also, I'm in someone else's territory and there are customs to obey.*'

I took that in, accepting that my pets had lives and concerns that were beyond my ability to comprehend.

'Were they friendly?' I asked her.

She licked her paw and wiped it around her ear. '*To a point.*'

I wasn't sure what that meant, but Buster had something to say. '*Cats are not friendly,*' he stated firmly. '*Cats do that which meets their needs or furthers their aims. They will help another cat only if it suits them to do so.*'

That Amber didn't argue was as good as her agreeing wholeheartedly with his thoughts on the matter. He made them sound like politicians.

'Amber would you be able to find the cat who was in the room when Quentin died? There was a cat under the bed. Describe it for her Buster.'

Buster pulled a thoughtful face, and his eyes rolled upward as his memory engaged. *'It was a mangy grey tabby, with a tatty ear and a big scar along its jawline. Two toes from its front left paw were missing and had been replaced by pieces of saw blade ...'*

'Buster.' I scowled at him.

'Its left eye was bionic?' he tried weakly.

I continued to scowl. 'An accurate description, please.'

Harrumphing, Buster plopped down so his head joined his belly on the carpet. It made him look like a deflated hairy Spacehopper. *'It was a young female cat. Maybe just more than a year old. It was jet black with green eyes and a small white smudge on her right rear flank.'*

Amber sniggered. *'Did she make you run away yelping like a puppy? I bet she did, didn't she?'*

'Can you find her?' I asked, cutting over Amber before she could rile Buster any further. 'I want to know what she heard or saw or smelled.'

Amber licked her paw again. *'What's in it for me?'*

Here we were again. Amber would do it, but she was quite mercenary when she wanted to be.

'If you want poached mackerel, you will have to wait until we get home. Otherwise, I will have to see what they have here.'

'The poached mackerel will do,' she let me know. *'I will see what I can do.'*

'Do you even know how to find the cats?' I asked, frowning because I was yet to even see one.

Amber stopped licking her paw, the task of washing her face seemingly complete. '*Oh, yes.*'

That was all I got, for in the next moment, she jumped nimbly down from the bed, accidentally on purpose landing on Buster's back.

My Bulldog reacted as one might expect, leaping to his feet to chase the cat, but Amber was way too fast. Before Buster could get his paws moving, she had crossed the room, but she wasn't heading for the door, she was trotting toward the fireplace.

It wasn't lit, of course, it was ornamental now as the building had central heating fitted, but as I watched, she jumped into the hearth and vanished.

Buster arrived at the fireplace a second later.

'Where'd she go?' I asked, joining him, and kneeling down to peer inside.

'What's going on, Auntie?' Mindy wanted to know, coming back into my room from the hallway outside to find me with my head in the fireplace and Buster under my chest as we both craned our necks to see where the cat might have got to.

Reversing out once more, I had my lips pursed. 'There's one of those secret passages in here.'

'Cor, where?' Mindy rushed to look for herself.

More athletic and supple than me, she clambered into the flue to get a better look. What we could see when we looked at the hearth was a brick wall at the back. There was a gap to the left though. It wasn't visible unless you were looking for it.

Mindy pushed herself back to upright. 'This is what Mr Benton was saying about the gaps in the wall the original owner had for his cats. What a strange thing to do.'

Buster told her, *'Felicity sent that daft cat to find out what the other cats know.'* His tone made it clear he would not be happy if she were able to return with useful information.

'What did he say?' Mindy asked. That she couldn't understand him disappointed her immensely.

'I sent Amber to find the cat who was in the room where Quentin died. I'm hoping it might have heard or seen something.'

Mindy nodded her head enthusiastically. 'Cat spies. That's a great idea.' As if suddenly remembering why she was in my room, she said, 'Mr Benton asked me to get you. He thinks they have everyone assembled.'

Volunteered

People were assembled in the ballroom. The route to it and the ballroom itself was decorated with flowers – many thousands of pounds worth because this was to be the main room in which the ceremony would take place. I observed the handiwork of the florists, nodding my head at their efforts as we neared the doors.

The murmur of conversation beyond them was easy to hear in the quiet house. So too the storm raging outside.

Mindy got to the doors first, pulling them both open in the centre so Buster and I could pass through. The buzz of chatter died as heads turned to see who was joining them. There could be no more than thirty people in the room, the sum total of everyone currently staying on Raven Island. Some of them had not intended to still be here, of course, I spotted the logo of a catering firm on the back of a jacket. The florists would be staying locally – in a B&B on the mainland would be my guess – as they would still be decorating tomorrow, plus handing out buttonholes for the male guests and posies for the ladies.

The only people visibly absent were Anton and Geoffrey, who already knew about the body – obviously, and were settling into their new room.

Mindy nudged my arm, squeaking quietly but excitedly as she flashed her eyes around the room. 'There are so many celebs here, Auntie!'

I gave her a sort of half shrug. 'There almost always are at my weddings, Mindy. You know that.'

'Yes, Auntie, but this time they are cool celebs. That's Nat Spanks from *Cheater's Palace!*' she gushed.

I knew the woman she referred to only because it was my job to do so. I had never watched *Cheater's Palace*, believing it to be a gawdy, tasteless reality TV show in which couples had their fidelity needlessly tested by introducing better looking partners for them to spend time with. Nat Spanks was the presenter, and one of those surgically enhanced women with boobs so big they looked likely to give her a balance problem.

Boris, the owner of Raven's Bluff, was holding audience, standing apart from everyone else at the front of the ballroom where tomorrow the head table would be positioned.

He cleared his throat to get everyone's attention. 'Ladies and gentlemen, most of you no doubt are wondering why we requested you to all assemble here. The short answer is that there has been a death.' His announcement sent a ripple around the room, people gasping or muttering shocked expletives. 'The death,' Boris continued, 'appears to be suspicious.'

'*It was murder!*' barked Buster, who thankfully couldn't be understood by anyone but me.

I dropped to one knee to shush him, but when I got there, I had a better idea. Speaking quietly, I said, 'Go, Buster. Use your nose. See if you can find the man who left his scent on Quentin's clothes.'

Buster wagged his tail, the little stub flicking back and forth in excitement as he trotted off around the room. Would he find the killer instantly? What would I do if Buster found someone and started barking? A second ago, I'd thought it was a good idea, now I was not so sure, but it was too late to stop my dog who was already moving between the wedding guests as they listened to what Boris had to say.

'What do you mean by suspicious?' asked Harold Cambridge. He was the new boyfriend of Geoffrey's former wife. I made no comment about her attending but the difficult divorce she and Geoffrey finally completed only weeks ago was one which had made all the papers. It was anything but peaceful, and it surprised me to see her here.

The tabloids gave the impression the former husband and wife hated each other. Geoffrey had caught the worst of their attention, the press writing stories in which he was accused of many infidelities and there were fame hungry men who came out of the woodwork to claim they were a former lover of the TV star. How much of what made it into print was true … well, who could guess. I suspected at least some of it would be.

Boris didn't answer for a second, and I thought he was going to avoid the question until he started talking.

'The wedding photographer, a man called Quentin Falstaff, was found hanging in the honeymoon suite. There was a suicide note which would indicate that he took his own life.'

'So what makes you think it wasn't suicide,' demanded another man. I had to crane my neck to see who it was, spotting one of the best men – each groom had one. This one was Edward Tolly, Anton's agent and close confidant.

Again Boris looked like he was struggling for words, and without planning to, I found myself talking.

'The handwriting did not match examples we found in his room and I spoke with Quentin just a short while before he was found. He was not suicidal,' I stated boldly.

'In your opinion,' pointed out Harold argumentatively.

As if he hadn't spoken, I continued what I was saying, 'He was seen shortly before he died and did not have a rope with him.'

'He fetched it after he was seen,' argued Harold with a bored sigh.

'His camera, which he never went anywhere without, is yet to be found.'

'Have you checked his room?' Harold asked, all but laughing at my imagined incompetence.

I turned to face him, failing to keep the frown from my face. 'Yes, thank you. His laptop is missing too. That's another item he never went anywhere without because he had it custom built with a huge memory for all the pictures.' Harold held my gaze, returning my annoyed glare with one of his own. 'I believe Quentin was murdered.'

A second ripple of gasps and murmurs went around the room, but Harold Cambridge felt prompted to argue even further.

'Oh, please. What is this? Amateur sleuth hour? Call the police, get the coroner, and next time you feel like dragging me from my room to listen to your nonsense ... don't.'

Buster bared his teeth. *'Is it okay if I bite him?'*

'What is your issue?' asked Mindy, getting riled.

'Do you hear the storm outside?' I asked my challenger.

Before he could answer, a fresh, yet familiar voice piped up. It was Eric again. 'There'll be no police here today, sonny,' he cackled.

Instantly ushered into silence by Ellis Carter, Boris went on to explain to everyone present that the causeway was shut off by the tide and no boats would be able to get here until the storm dissipates.

'We are stuck here,' I pointed out, letting the words sink in. 'And so is Quentin's killer.'

'If indeed he was killed,' argued Harold yet again. Then, deciding he needed to take no further part in whatever everyone else was doing, he grabbed his partner's hand and began to tug her toward the doors. 'Come on, Emma. We have champagne getting warm and much better things to do than waste our time on this rubbish.'

Emma let him tug her forward a few feet before speaking for the first time.

'But what if there is a killer here?' she wanted to know as she dug her heels in.

Lightning flashed to fill the windows with blinding light and another peel of thunder made it so no one heard what Harold said in reply. However, I could see from his face that he was angry with her and so too could everyone else in the room.

He tugged at her arm again, hooking her elbow to try to force her to go with him. 'Come along, Emma, you are showing me up,' he joked, teasingly, but it sounded like a warning to me.

From outside the ballroom came the sound of my grooms approaching. They were talking at normal volume, their voices loud enough for everyone in the ballroom to hear since we were all silent as we watched the uncomfortable display unfold.

The man nearest to Harold and Emma was the one from the catering firm. He was a young man but broad and muscular. I expected him to intervene, but instead he seemed to fade into the background, stepping backwards to merge with the people behind him.

Everyone had that nervous look on their faces – they thought perhaps someone ought to intervene but were hoping it wouldn't have to be them.

Before anyone could, Harold sensed all eyes were on him, and dropped his grip on Emma's arm. He was biting his lip, clearly not saying that which he wanted to. Stepping back, he wiped a hand across his brow, shot his girlfriend a rage-filled grimace, and strode from the room. Amplified by the quiet, his footsteps sounded loud on the wooden floorboards.

Emma's cheeks were bright red, and she didn't seem to have anyone to turn to for comfort. Most people had backed away, and just as I thought she was going to bolt from the room in her embarrassment, the most unlikely person stepped in – her ex-husband.

Geoffrey came into the ballroom with Anton, both men looking over their shoulders at Harold's departing back. They had curious looks on their faces, probably because they'd just seen the rage on Harold's. However, seeing her ex arrive, Emma ran to him with tears on her cheeks and Geoffrey pulled her into a hug. I guess they had a lot of mutual memories and not all were bad. Maybe the papers had exaggerated the acrimonious nature of their divorce. I couldn't know, but my attention was drawn away from them by a question.

'What do we do then?' asked Nat Spanks, a woman used to being the centre of attention. 'If we cannot call the police, what do we do?'

'We investigate ourselves,' said Mindy, excitement making her eyes glow. 'Aunt Felicity is a dab hand at the old amateur sleuthing.' Now everyone was looking at my niece.

'Shhh,' I hissed at her.

People were looking for her to expand, so that was what she did, ignoring my pleas for her to stop talking.

'Auntie was the one who stopped the killer at Loxton Hall.'

'You mean the Sashatastic wedding debacle?' Gazelle Hubbard wanted to confirm.

Mindy squeaked again because the person she thought of as a celeb had spoken to her. 'That's right! It was this crazy woman posing as the caterer.'

'*I broke her ankles*,' boasted Buster proudly, arriving back at my side. I had to assume he'd drawn a blank on the scent he went looking for.

Gazelle looked genuinely impressed by Mindy's claims about me. So did many others who were all staring my way and making me feel very uncomfortable.

'I guess we'll leave it all to you, then,' Nat Spanks said to a round of agreement.

I found my voice. 'I'm just a wedding planner,' I blurted.

Mindy argued. 'Auntie you are THE wedding planner. That's what you are always telling people. Besides,' she dropped her voice and came close enough that she could whisper to me without everyone else hearing, 'think of all the publicity solving another murder will bring.'

'Yes,' I scoffed. 'Bad publicity. I will become a pariah, getting shunned by prospective couples for fear their nuptials will be a bloodbath.'

Nat Spanks wasn't to be put off though. 'All in favour of having the wedding planner find the killer please raise your hands.'

Every hand in the room reached for the sky.

I swore inside my head.

Buster barked, *'Yeah! It's Devil Dog time!'*

Mindy whooped her excitement, and I hung my head, sighing and wondering how I was going to get out of this mess now.

A Terrible Sleuth

'You could have just said, *No*,' Mindy pointed out stubbornly.

We were back in my room where I could be less than pleased without anyone else seeing me.

'Could I?' I snapped back at her grumpily. 'The grooms, for whom I currently work, both put their hands up. They want me to work out who killed Quentin. So too did Boris Benton, the owner of this house. So too did everyone else, and must I remind you that every guest at one of my weddings is a potential future customer. There is ...'

'... no better advertising than giving the guests the best experience they have ever enjoyed,' Mindy finished my sentence, repeating a saying I drummed into her months ago. 'So what do we do then, Auntie? The guests are now expecting us to investigate.'

I had been giving that exact question my undivided attention ever since Mindy did such a great job of volunteering me.

'We investigate,' I told her.

Mindy bounced on the spot, clapping her hands tother, 'Yay!'

Buster barked and spun like he does when he's chasing his tail.

'But we don't really,' I added.

'Huh?' Mindy stopped bouncing.

I gave her a what-can-I-tell-you expression. 'I don't know how to investigate a murder, Mindy. I'm a wedding planner. Catching Tarquin was a total accident. I didn't know it was him until after I made a complete fool of myself at the hospital if you remember.'

She grimaced. 'Yeah, you kinda did do that.'

'Yes,' I agreed unhappily, remembering how mortified I'd felt accusing perfectly innocent people. 'And I didn't catch Chablis either,' I reminded Mindy. 'She caught me is a more accurate way of looking at it. If Vince hadn't come along, she would have killed me.'

'*Hold on*,' whined Buster. '*I saved you from Chablis.*'

I crouched to pat him and ruffle the fur under his chin. 'You were very helpful, Buster,' I assured him. He keeled over onto his side so I could get to his belly. Looking back up at my niece, I continued what I had been saying. 'My point is that I didn't solve anything. I was a terrible sleuth. If I investigate here, I am more likely to trample on the evidence the police will need to catch the killer. They will come as soon as the storm dies down. In the meantime, we will make it look as though we are doing what we can to identify Quentin's killer.'

Mindy skewed her lips to one side. 'Okay, Auntie.'

'Please bear in mind we have a major wedding with hundreds of guests tomorrow. The storm will pass, the guests will arrive, and we will need to be ready to do everything we came here to do but in a compressed timespan. It will not be easy.'

'Yes, Auntie.' Mindy looked a little cowed, but it lasted no more than a heartbeat before her usual exuberant nature took over again. 'So what do we do first?' she wanted to know.

My answer was to pose a question to Buster.

'I take it you didn't find anyone with the scent you could smell on Quentin?'

I was scratching his belly, right at the end of his ribcage and he was flopped on the carpet with his eyes closed and a blissful look while his back left leg twitched spasmodically. I had to stop and repeat my question before I got an answer.

'*Nah, no one. I did smell the woman though.*'

'The one you said you could smell in the honeymoon suite?' I tried to confirm.

Buster wagged his tail. '*S'right. She was in the ballroom with everyone else.*'

I rolled my eyes. 'Why didn't you say?'

Buster frowned at me and sounded grumpy when he said, '*You asked me to find the man who left his scent on Quentin. I only have one nose.*'

I cut the argument off and focused on the solution. 'Okay so who was it?'

Buster raised one eyebrow. '*It was the woman who smelled of the same thing,*' he tried, speaking slowly as if talking to an idiot.

'Can't you describe her?' I begged, beginning to feel a little exasperated.

'*I can describe the smell,*' he offered helpfully. Then, seeing the expression on my face, switched to snarky. '*Look, all you humans look alike to a dog. We can tell the difference between young and old, male and female, but mostly we pay attention to what you smell of just to see if you are carrying food. That's not all that easy though because you sneaky blighters have a habit of putting your food inside packets to disguise its odour.*'

I rolled my eyes again. This was not the first time I had endured this conversation. Buster believed we put crisps, cakes, chocolate bars, and other treats in packets purely so dogs could not smell them. He refused to entertain the idea that we did it for convenience of handling, preservation et cetera.

With a defeated huff, I tried to narrow down who the mystery woman might be.

'Was she old or young?'

Buster replied without needing to think. *'Neither.'*

I had to guess that placed her in the thirty to sixty bracket – hardly narrowing the field.

'Was she fat or thin?'

Buster didn't know the answer to that one, nor to the next half a dozen about hair colour, what she was wearing, and if he remembered her shoes.

I knew we could try again, but I wasn't sure what I would do with the information even if Buster could single out one person. She might have a legitimate reason for being in the room or maybe she was in there long before anything happened to Quentin.

I chose to let it go, filing it away to consider later. I thought I might ask Geoffrey and Anton about it, but if they wanted to know how I knew, I couldn't tell them Buster could smell her. How could I explain that?

Going back to a question Mindy posed about what I planned to do next if I was going to make it look like I was investigating, I told her that we should get some of the wedding guests involved. That way I wouldn't be doing all the work. I was curious to see if we could find Quentin's camera and laptop. Those were the only things I could immediately spot as missing from his room. There might be other things, but someone had taken them and maybe the reason for that had something to do with why Quentin was dead. I was going to recruit Ellis Carter, the house manager, and ask him to drum up some more help to search the house.

Honestly, I didn't hold out much hope for finding the missing items even if they were still on the premises – the house was vast. I was also curious to find out if we really had accounted for everyone. Was it possible that the killer had come to the island but wasn't among those who congregated in the ballroom? Was it someone who followed Quentin here?

Before we left the room, I poked my head into the fireplace again, holding onto the mantlepiece for balance as I stretched my head inside the hearth.

'Amber,' I called loudly. My voice echoed in the darkness, but no response came back. 'Amber.' I waited a few seconds, told myself to stop worrying because she would be fine, and pulled myself back to upright again.

'*No answer?*' Buster sought to confirm.

I shook my head, grabbing a jacket to slip over my shoulders for the temperature seemed to have dropped a few degrees. 'No. No answer. I'm sure she is fine.'

Buster sucked some air between his teeth. '*Oh, I don't know. A posh cat like Amber among all those scraggly kitties living in the walls. Her presence might be considered to be an intrusion. They might not take too kindly to that. She's probably dead already.*'

I frowned at him. 'Buster, that is not a very nice thing to say.'

Buster looked surprised. 'There's a silver lining, don't forget.'

'Such as?'

Buster sniggered. '*I just told you – she's probably dead already!*' He thought he was quite the comedian.

Thinking I ought to swat his bottom yet knowing he wouldn't even feel it if I did, I picked up my handbag and started for the door.

I found Mr Carter in a small office at the front of the house just off the main entrance lobby.

He was accommodating to my request. 'Of course, Mrs Philips. I will see what help I can drum up. There are a few people gathered in the ballroom – those who were due to return to the mainland but are now trapped here such as the florists and that chap from your catering firm.'

'We can ask the wedding guests if they are prepared to muck in too,' I told him. 'I will ask them myself.' They were here to eat, drink, and celebrate, but I hoped some might volunteer to help. These were extreme circumstances, after all.

I thought about roping in the chefs as well. Two had come early to receive the food and make sure everything was in order. Then I remembered they also needed to prepare an evening meal for everyone on the island and dismissed them from my list of potential helpers.

Before Ellis could scurry away, I said, 'We need to divide them up, so they know which part of the house to check. Otherwise, they might all search the same bit.'

'Good point,' he agreed. However, he then stopped in the doorway. 'It's kind of a big house,' he pointed out. 'Even if they search all night, they won't be able to cover that much of it. If someone hid the laptop and camera it could be anywhere.'

I already knew this; my efforts were intended as a token effort to save face. While I knew that meant I was messing people around unnecessarily, I hadn't been able to come up with anything else yet.

I was going to ask him another question when a scream ripped through the air.

Rising Body Count

Buster barked, making me jump yet again. He waddle/turned around to face back into the house for that is where the sound came from. It was a woman's voice this time, but the sense of horror the scream contained was no different from the one we heard Anton emit an hour ago.

Ellis took off running. So too Mindy, her long legs powering her across the lobby and into the central hub of the great house.

Buster, off the lead because I didn't feel there was a need for it indoors, chased after them.

As he got up to full speed, I heard him bark, *'Dun, dun, DAH!'* I had no idea what that was supposed to signify and wasn't going to ask.

Mindy's voice drifted back to me as I did my best to keep them in sight. 'Come on, Auntie!'

Chasing after Ellis, Mindy, and Buster, I got that odd feeling of being watched. I turned my head, still running but looking over my shoulders. I expected to find someone behind me but found only empty hallway.

I used to be really fit. That is, my memory is that I used to be really fit. I was a ballerina for a while and had to weigh nothing and have strong muscles. To keep my weight down, I ran rather than avoid eating, which is the tactic a lot of the girls employed. It meant I got fit, but now well into my fifties, I hadn't run for anything other than a bus in over a decade and it was showing.

Mercifully, Buster wasn't built for running either and when he started to get out of breath, I caught up with him. We both decided to walk. We would get there, but I was in no hurry, for whatever it was that had made the lady scream, it most likely wasn't something I wanted to see.

I was right.

To find the latest scene of drama, all I had to do was use my ears and follow the sound of raised voices. Raven's Bluff is a maze of corridors and rooms, some of which just seemed to lead to more corridors and rooms. I found myself at the top of a small flight of stairs and went down them to find a gaggle of people gathered in the passageway at the bottom.

I could tell I was nearly there just from the increasing level of noise and the clarity of the words because I could now make out what people were saying.

'So who is he?' asked Mindy.

Whether her question was aimed at Ellis Carter or not, he was the one who answered. 'I don't know. He looks vaguely familiar, like I met him recently, but I don't know him.'

There was a press of people blocking my view. I recognised them all. Two were the florists I hired in to decorate the house, and two more were minor celebrities and guests at the wedding. They probably wished they arrived late and got stuck on the mainland now. Their names – I had to dredge them from my memory – were Ian Riggs, a reality TV star who first appeared on a singing contest, and Ryan Clarke, who was his boyfriend and a TV gardener known for having a ripped physique. He made a point of appearing topless on his shows.

Ryan and Ian were on the floor, kneeling and doing something.

The something they were doing, I discovered when I got close enough, was reviving a woman who had fainted. It was Hattie, the homophobic old lady from earlier. She was flat on the carpet but had someone's rolled up coat under her head. She looked white as a sheet.

I saw why when I moved just a little closer. There was a body in the closet behind her. A pair of feet were sticking out into the hallway. They were devoid of shoes and socks, and when I tracked the legs upward, I discovered the man to be clad only in his undershorts.

The people in the hallway were engaged in checking Hattie was going to be all right, or they were discussing who the latest dead person might be. There could be no doubt he was dead; his eyes were open, staring up at the ceiling without seeing anything and there was a cruel bruise around his throat. I would never claim to know what I was looking at, but to my eyes the man had been strangled.

'Where does this corridor go?' I asked, swinging attention in my direction.

Ellis answered, 'Outside. There are no more rooms before you get to the door. Then it's the garage and car parking area just across the way.'

'And no one knows who this is?' I asked.

I got a sea of blank faces in response. I had a dead photographer, murdered by goodness knows who for goodness knows what reason, and now a mystery man in the house who no one could identify.

'I'll see if there is anything in the closet,' Mindy volunteered. 'Maybe his wallet is in there.' She wrinkled her nose, looking down at the nearly naked form. 'It might be under him, I suppose.'

I didn't like how excited she sounded at the prospect of touching the body. Her mother and I didn't see eye to eye anyway. If Mindy were to let slip what she got up to this weekend, my sister would insist it was all my fault.

'I should do that,' volunteered Ellis, chivalrously, but Mindy was already there.

Over her shoulder as she clambered over and around the man, she said, 'I've got it.' She drew a blank though, standing up and declaring there was nothing to be found.

The man was in his late twenties; that was my best guess. He had long, wavy dark brown hair pulled into a top knot and there was a line around his skull where a hat might have rested. There wasn't much to remark on about his appearance, other than he was skinny. His nose had a kink in it, as if broken once and never set properly afterward. There were no obvious scars, and I could see no tattoos. The police would be able to identify him, I felt certain of that, but for now he remained a mystery.

Why was he naked? Where were his clothes? It was far too cool to entertain moving around the house without layers on. Was he a guest at the house? He wasn't anyone from the guest list – I would know his face if he were. If he wasn't staying here, then he had to be a delivery driver or someone who was here because of the wedding. If that was the case, then the question about his clothes remained.

'Mindy, can you take a picture, please?' I begged of her. She was nearest.

Her phone made a shutter clicking noise, artificial of course, just to let the person know the camera had done its thing.

I blew out a frustrated breath. Two bodies in just over an hour and people were looking to me to work out who was behind it.

'We need to call the police again,' I declared, wishing the storm would pass.

Ellis sucked on his teeth. 'We need to tell everyone there has been a second murder too.'

He wasn't wrong.

Hattie chose that moment to sit up. Ian Riggs gave her a hand to get upright, and she came to sit with her legs tucked around her a little.

'What were you doing down here, Hattie?' I asked, the question popping into my head.

She looked around and up at me. 'There was a cold breeze. Someone left the door open. It gets terribly cold in the house if there are doors left open. I could hear it banging in the wind, so I came down to shut it. When I came back this way,' she indicated her direction of travel with one hand, 'I spotted the closet door open. It wouldn't shut properly, so I opened it to see what was inside and that's when I ... well, he was inside.' She didn't turn her head to look at the corpse still lying against the mops and brooms inside.

A voice called along the corridor behind me; Eric was on his way to find his wife.

It broke the spell I was under and made me want to get my feet moving. As Ellis helped Hattie to her feet, I asked him, 'Where can we put him? We need to keep him preserved for the police, but we can't just leave him lying here sticking out of a closet. Do you have somewhere cold?'

'The chiller in the kitchen?' he suggested.

Mindy said, 'Ewwww. No one is going to want to eat tomorrow if you do that.'

She made a valid point.

'Somewhere else?' I asked.

Thinking Like a Detective

The somewhere else turned out to be the cellar, which was about as creepy a place as I could have imagined. It was filled with cobwebs – which I do not like at the best of times – and I swear I heard something skittering away in the dark. The sound made me shudder.

Buster had been left on the ground level with Mindy which was a good thing because he might have run off into the dark chasing whatever it was otherwise.

Light in the cellar came from bare light bulbs, though there were only just enough to beat the gloom back a few feet. It was going to require a lot more of them to scare the eerie darkness away.

Ian Riggs and Ryan Clarke were good enough to volunteer to help move the body. I guess they didn't feel it was okay to leave Mindy and me to deal with him. Ellis found another sheet to put over the mystery man's body. They made a makeshift stretcher from a door and carried him down to the cellar where they laid him on the dusty floor and backed away. I all but ran to get back upstairs and into the light.

From there, we returned to the ballroom where Hattie was the centre of attention and nursing what looked like a glass of neat whisky.

The bar at the side of the ballroom was doing a rather brisk trade. It wasn't set up as a bar for paying guests of course, Raven's Bluff isn't a hotel or wedding venue, but Boris had turned it over for my team to use for the weekend and it had already been stocked, the drinks paid for in advance by the grooms.

The early guests were making good use of it even though the bar staff were yet to arrive. The florists were there, so too the delivery driver from the catering firm. They were all trapped on the island until the storm passed. I knew Ellis was organising rooms for them among the many other things he needed to do.

'What's next?' asked Buster, doing his rasping, deep voice. 'Shall we shake down a few of the shadier looking ones? I bet they know more than they are letting on. Give me a few minutes in a room with them and I'll get 'em to talk.'

'What's he saying?' whispered Mindy.

With a sigh, I replied, 'Nothing sensible.' His question about what to do next was pertinent though. I might not want to be the one playing detective, but my desire to act as if I were until the police showed up was already beginning to fray. There was a second body. It's not the sort of thing one can ignore.

Everyone knew about it too, Hattie's arrival in the ballroom ensured that word spread.

Edward Tolley spotted me as I came into the room and rushed to intercept my path.

'Is it true?' he asked. 'Has here been a second murder?' He looked like he already knew it was true but just didn't want to believe it. If he was hoping to get a different report from me, he was to be disappointed.

'Yes, Edward, I'm afraid so.'

His question drew the crowd of people away from Hattie, a gaggle of them rushing to hear what I had to say.

One of Geoffrey's on-screen family got in his question first, 'The old lady said the man was strangled. Who is it?'

I was about to say I didn't know, when it occurred to me that this was precisely what I needed. Someone here had to recognise our mystery guest.

I touched Mindy's arm. 'Have you got that photograph?'

Surprised by my request, Mindy dug in the pocket of her stretchy leggings. 'Sure.'

Before she could show anyone, I pointed out, 'I need to ask you all to have a look at the picture of the man's face. So far no one knows who it is. I must warn you it is not a nice photograph.'

My warning caused several grimaces, but no one tried to get away – they were all too curious to see who the dead man was. A rough head count told me I had about half the island's residents in front of me.

Tentatively, Mindy turned her phone over to show the awful picture.

There were a few, 'Oh, my goodnesses,' and a few quietly uttered expletives but no one recognised the dead man. His face was horrible to look at, but Mindy got a good shot which made it easy to see his features. I'd watched the faces as people came forward to get a good look and none of them reacted in a way that made me want to question if they were lying.

The last person to take a look was the delivery driver from the catering firm. He didn't come forward like most other people in the room; he was skulking in a corner and doing his best to not be noticed. Like the florists, he was stuck here due to unfortunate timing. He ought to have been able to make his delivery and easily return to the mainland. The storm cut him off when it closed the causeway an hour earlier than expected.

I couldn't blame him for not wanting to look – dead people are gruesome and remind us of our own mortality. I also doubted he would have any idea who the dead man was, but I felt a need to be thorough if I was going to do this at all.

'Can you look at this picture, please?' Mindy smiled at him.

He was a handsome young man in his early twenties. I hadn't seen him before today but had to concede that I did not know all the staff employed by Barry, my chief catering supplier. Standing a couple of inches over six feet tall, he had light brown, almost blonde hair which was buzz cut to a uniform length on the bits I could see. He wore a catering company ballcap on his head to hide the rest of it. He was muscular, his bulky physique easy to see beneath his clothes which barely fit in some places. The material covering his thighs and upper arms was stretched to breaking point.

Mindy had noticed him too, holding up her phone for him to see and smiling at him in an engaging way. She clearly liked what she saw.

Diligently, if a little reluctantly, he peered at the picture. I tried to watch his face but the company ballcap he wore with the caterer's logo on it hid his face when he bent forward to get close to the phone. He looked thoughtful when he stood up again.

'He looks like my Cousin Robert, but ... sorry, I don't know him. You say even the staff don't know who he is?'

I shook my head. 'We still have some people to show him to. He couldn't have been here by accident. Someone has to know who he is.'

The man nodded. 'I'm sure you're right. Could he be the one who killed the first victim?' he asked, dropping his voice so everyone in the room wouldn't hear.

I could only shrug. 'Then who killed him?' I pointed out the glaring hole in his theory.

I got a goofy grin in return. 'Good point. Say, if you ladies need a hand with the investigation … they were asking for volunteers to help search the house earlier, I'm only too happy to help out. It's not like I can go with my original plan for this evening. The lads will have to go out looking for foxy ladies without me,' he shot another grin at Mindy and winked, his intention to flirt with her open and obvious.

Ellis Carter came into the room with Boris Benton at his side. Boris looked troubled, the second murder hitting him harder than the first. I locked eyes with Ellis, asking a question with my expression.

I got a short shake of his head – The homeowner didn't know the man either.

As the delivery driver wandered away, Mindy touched my shoulder and asked a question.

'When we tried to account for everyone earlier, that man never came up. I guess that's no surprise if no one knows who he is, but he was down near the door that leads to the cars. Do you think maybe one of the cars outside is his? It might have some information in it to help us identify the owner.'

That was great thinking. Why hadn't I come up with that?

Across the room, Boris was pouring himself a large shot of bourbon. I needed to speak with him before I did anything else.

I had to wait while he downed his glass and poured another. He had his back to me and didn't appear to have noticed I was standing in his shadow. I tapped his shoulder.

'Boris,' he jerked as if startled – the man was on edge. 'Sorry,' I apologised as he spun around to face me.

'Felicity,' the master of the house gasped. 'You gave me such a fright. Is everything all right? You haven't come to tell me there's a third body, have you?'

'Goodness, no,' I stuttered, horrified by the idea. 'I just wanted to speak to you about a few things.'

'Such as?'

'Well, for a start I think we need to get Hattie and Eric to one side. They are mingling with the wedding guests, several of whom are homosexual. I do not want them spewing any more of their filth. Can you see to it that they are somewhere else, please?'

Mindy said, 'I thought you were dismissing them, Mr Benton.'

To me, he said, 'I will have them removed from the ballroom.' Then to Mindy, he replied, 'I am yet to officially dismiss them. Given their disposition, I will not be surprised if they create havoc when I tell them so I'm leaving it until the causeway opens again. I'll tell them then and have Ellis escort them from the island.'

'Don't they live here?' I asked, a little confused.

Boris blew out a frustrated sigh. 'They do. I got them when I bought the place and it seemed unfair to turf them out just because they were grumpy and a bit lazy.'

'What do they even do?' asked Mindy.

'Not a lot,' replied Boris with a tired laugh. 'Hattie was the housekeeper and Eric the butler when I arrived a decade ago, but it was clear they were already too old for the job. I pay them enough to keep them going and they live here for free in a set of rooms at the back by the kitchen.'

I felt Mindy was right when she said, 'That sounds like a sweet deal.'

To move the conversation along, I said, 'Mindy and I will be doing what we can to figure out who the mystery man is and what happened to Quentin. Can I please leave it to you to see Eric and Hattie are moved along?' I shot a glance at the old lady, who was being attended to even now by Ian Riggs and his boyfriend. Maybe she just hadn't realised they were a couple. 'Maybe give her a few more minutes,' I suggested, not wanting to turf the old woman out when she still looked to be in shock.

Boris sipped his drink. 'I can see that it is done.' With a free hand, he motioned for Ellis to join us. 'Anything else?'

I nodded. 'Yes. Unless someone identifies the dead man, he will remain an enigma. Mindy had an idea about the cars outside though. Can you get someone to go around to everyone and have them jot down which car is theirs? Model and registration number should do it. If we have one left over, it has to be his.'

Boris nodded his understanding, his eyes on Ellis when he said, 'It will be done.'

'Thank you.' I took out my phone. It was time to call the police.

Someone in the Dark

When Ellis called the police an hour ago, he'd been put through to a detective sergeant with the last name Khan. He got a number to call back on and it was that number I dialled now. I'd taken myself out of the ballroom and across the hall to a narrow corridor. I could see the guests still, but it was quiet enough where I was to believe I was not being overheard.

'DS Khan,' a rough, man's voice resounded in my left ear. It had an impatient edge to it, like the man was already stressed and being asked to do too many things. The roughness made me think he smoked cigars and drank whisky but that was probably just me romanticising his job. In my head I could see him in black and white with a trilby or fedora hat like some private eye from the forties.

Shaking my head to clear the image, I said, 'Hello. This is Felicity Philips on Raven Island. You spoke with Ellis Carter a short while ago when he reported the death of Quentin Falstaff.' Introduction delivered, I waited for his cogs to turn. In that brief moment before the detective spoke again, I got the same feeling of being watched.

I whipped my head around, certain I was going to catch someone spying on me but yet again there was no one there.

DS Khan said, 'Yes. We are still looking to get out to the island as soon as the weather improves.'

I bit my lip, wondering what he would say to my next line. 'There's been another murder.'

I got silence for a beat. 'Another murder? I thought Mr Falstaff hanged himself.'

Not beating around the bush, I told him, 'It looks more likely that he was murdered. There are a number of obvious discrepancies.'

'Mr Carter claimed as much earlier. However, I have to withhold judgement until I have a coroner's report, Mrs Philips. What about the second body?'

I took a second to consult my brain, questioning whether I was seeing killers where there were none. 'It's a Caucasian man in his late twenties. I can send you a picture. No one knows who he is. At least, so far no one has admitted that they recognise him. One of the members of staff found him stuffed roughly inside a cleaning closet and if I had to guess, I would say he had been strangled.'

I could hear DS Khan making noises with his tongue as he processed the information. 'Stuffed into a closet, eh? It doesn't sound like an accident, I'll give you that. Look, I'm going to contact the coastguard and see if they can get me out to you. I can't promise anything, but it would be remiss of me to ignore the possibility that you have a killer on the island.'

I gulped. 'I think we do. The timings of the two deaths suggest whoever did it is still here, cut off by the storm tide.'

'Just sit tight, Mrs Philips. I'll call you back on this number when I can tell you more. I'll get to you if I can. Just don't move the bodies, okay?'

'Um.'

'Um?' he repeated my fumbled start of a sentence.

'Well, the body in the closet was … we didn't just want to leave it there.'

The detective made a frustrated noise. 'Okay. So where is it?'

'We put it in the cellar.'

'Is there someone with it?'

'Goodness no,' I pulled a face even though he couldn't see it. 'It's dark and horrible down there. And there are rats, I think.'

'You've got to put it somewhere else!' DS Khan blurted urgently. 'The body will have evidence on it. If the killer is there, his best bet is to get the body now he knows you have discovered it and throw it into the sea! It might be that he stuffed it into the closet because someone disturbed him. Look, I'm just guessing, but you have to guard that body!'

I was already running, heading back to the cellar as fast as I could go. DS Khan's voice was still in my ear, but I wheezed, 'I'll call you back!' and disconnected before I was completely out of breath.

It never occurred to me to shout to the people in the ballroom and maybe get Mindy's attention or anyone's for that matter. Not until I was heading down the cold stone stairs and into the dark did I think to question what I was doing.

Too late now, I ploughed on, down into the cool, damp air beneath the great house. The lights were still on which was a good thing because I had no idea where the light switch might be. But hitting the bottom of the stairs, out of breath and feeling nervous to be sharing the dingy space with nothing but a dead man, I realised the lights probably hadn't been left on.

They'd been turned on by the man now running into the dark on the far side of the cellar!

Frozen for a second as fear gripped me, I then thoughtlessly gave chase.

'Hey!' Shouting at the retreating form, I started running. The silhouette was that of a large, broad-shouldered man in a suit. I only caught a fleeting glance before the darkness swallowed him, but just as my pace slowed, my brain questioning what the heck I thought I was doing, I heard footsteps on stairs ahead of me.

Whoever it was – the killer – I felt certain, had found another staircase. It hadn't occurred to me to question that there might be more than one way into the cellar in such a large house. In the next second, there was a banging noise that sounded like a door opening and a flash of daylight ahead accompanied by the sound of the storm raging outside.

Disobeying every gut reaction in my body, I carried on running, chasing after the man who had to have been in the cellar to do exactly as DS Khan suggested – tamper with the evidence.

The darkness engulfed me, making me slow down until I remembered the phone still clutched in my hand. Cursing myself, I flicked the torch function with a finger, bringing it to life. Instantly, the way ahead was bathed in a swathe of bright, white light and I could see the foot of the stairs.

Like the ones I descended, these were carved from stone as if hewn from the land itself when the foundations were dug. Maybe they were.

Panting, but forcing myself onward, I ran up them two at a time until I got to the top. A large door blocked my exit, and as I flung it open, it was ripped from my grip by the wind.

It opened directly to the outside!

Rain lashed at me, wind whipping my hair, and before I could take a breath, a huge wave hit the side of the island a hundred yards away and shot sea spray into the air to a height of a hundred feet or more. It was terrifying to see nature's power so intimately.

There was no sign of the man I'd chased, but escaping this way, he would be soaked now. It would make him easy to identify, but I would have to be quick. It took five attempts to get the door shut, the wind tearing it from my hands four times before I managed to time it right and catch a lull.

I paused to check the body as I went back across the cellar. The head was uncovered, and his right arm was hanging out to trail in the dust that covered the floor. The fingers of the right hand had ink on them.

Confused, I crouched for a better look.

That's when Buster chose to lick my bottom.

I shrieked in fright, my brain convinced the dead man had just touched me with his left hand while I examined the right. It jolted me so much I fell over, rolling in the cellar dirt, rat poop, and whatever else might be covering the floor.

'Wow!' exclaimed Mindy, her hand on her heart.

I was lying half on my back, half scrambling to get away from the menace behind me when the message that I was safe finally registered.

The delivery man was coming across the cellar floor behind Mindy with Boris, Irina Kalashnikov, Matt Finn, Nat Spanks, and a few others behind him.

'What the heck just happened?' asked Nat.

Mindy asked, 'Are you all right, Auntie?'

Buster wagged his tail ferociously and tried to climb onto my lap to lick my face. *'Hello, Felicity!'*

'I need new underwear,' I muttered mostly to myself, and quietly enough that only Mindy heard.

'You need a complete change of clothes,' she assured me. 'You are covered in dirt.'

A troop of other people arrived near the body, none of them wanted to get closer than a few yards.

'We saw you run by,' said the delivery driver. 'But we didn't see where you went.'

'Are you wet?' asked Nat Spanks.

I pushed myself back to upright, trying to dust myself off, but doing nothing other than smearing the muck around my clothes.

Mindy gave me a hand up, saying, 'I had to ask Buster to use his nose. He seems to understand everything.'

'That's right,' Buster wagged his tail. *'All dogs do. Mostly though we pretend we can't because it's more fun to keep our humans on their toes.'*

'I just got off the phone with a detective on the mainland. He said we needed to put the body somewhere safe because the killer might try to mess with it – to destroy evidence or something.' I was still out of breath, not helped by Buster making my heart stop when he licked me.

While I was trying to get my heartrate under control, Mindy said, 'I'll see if I can find Ellis. He must be able to lock the cellar doors.'

I took a gulp of air and carried on with what I had been saying, 'So I came to check but there was a man down here when I came in.'

'Who was it?' asked the delivery guy, tense excitement in his tone. His question was echoed by everyone else.

'No idea,' I admitted to the sound of disappointment. 'But he went out into the storm and I think he was wearing a suit. Whoever it was has to be soaked.' I spread my arms and looked down at my clothing to make a point. 'This is how wet I got in just a few seconds.'

Mindy pulled a face. 'Um, Auntie.' She darted a finger out, quickly drawing my attention down to my chest where I saw my top was plastered to my skin. I had two very obvious nipples poking through the fabric.

The delivery driver was doing his best to not look at my boobs while also making sure he got a good look. He wasn't the only guilty man in my immediate vicinity.

Pulling my jacket over my chest, and holding it there by folding my arms, I started back toward the stairs.

'We need to get everyone together and see who is missing. Someone just got soaked and that person is probably our killer.'

All of a sudden, I had a purpose to my gait. Someone killed two people, one of whom was a friend of mine and now I was going to be able to catch them. When DS Khan arrived, whether soon or tomorrow morning, I was going to have a solved case and criminal tied up with the very rope he used to murder Quentin.

'*I'll stay here and guard the body,*' barked Buster, making me pause. '*A dark cellar is exactly the right place for a justice seeker like Devil Dog to hang out. If you need me, I'll be brooding silently.*'

I looked at him for a second, locking eyes with my idiot Bulldog as I questioned whether I was going to have to carry him back upstairs just to get him to come. 'Buster, there are rats down here.'

He overtook me on the stairs.

Room to Room

Thankful to no longer be in the cellar, I was nevertheless beginning to feel the cold creeping into my bones from my wet clothing. I wasn't quite soaked through to my knickers, but I wasn't far off. However, my desire to get clean, warm, and dressed in new clothes was going to have to wait, the urgency of another task was taking priority.

It was as if I had an entourage as we made our way back through the house to the ballroom. Mindy and Buster were right by me, the delivery guy on the other side and all those who had followed them down to the cellar were right on our heels.

We met Ellis as he came down a flight of stairs.

'He's got a suit on!' cried Nat Spanks accusingly.

Ellis's eyes flared in question.

'It's not him,' I assured her. 'He's bone dry for a start and that's the same suit he's been wearing all day.'

'He's probably got more than one,' said the delivery driver.

It was a fair point.

'What's going on?' Ellis wanted to know, descending the last few stairs to join us at ground level.

Mindy piped up, 'Auntie saw someone in the cellar. They were fiddling with the mystery body and ran outside into the storm.'

'It was a man in a suit,' I explained a little more clearly. 'He was bigger than you, though. Much wider at the shoulder. Older too,' I recalled, searching my memory. Did the man I saw have grey hair or was that just the poor light in the cellar making it look that way.

Mindy asked, 'Can you lock the cellar doors?'

Ellis frowned at her question. 'I already did.'

'Well, someone opened them again,' I assured him. 'How many doors are there?'

'Just two,' Ellis looked perplexed. 'They were both open?'

I nodded, my mind trying to make a connection out of the new information. Someone opened the locked doors. Did that mean there was another person with keys? Were Eric and Hattie still in the ballroom? In the next instant, I dismissed them as suspects – the man I saw was not Eric.

Ellis wasn't sure what to make of what we were telling him but said, 'I have been going around to the last few people to ask about cars. I just need to double check because we may have one that is not accounted for.'

This was good news and it felt like we were closing the net. 'Super. I need to get everyone together again. Either the man I saw is still outside or he is trying to hide the fact that he was. Can you help me before you deal with the cars?'

Ellis looked thrilled at the prospect of catching the killer. 'Let's not waste any time,' he said, already hustling along the corridor.

'Yeah!' Mindy clapped her hands together. 'Let's get this sucker!'

Buster barked, *'Devil Dog volunteers to be the one to take him down. I'm going to run through his legs like they are a cat flap!'*

Bursting through the doors in a dramatic fashion, all eyes turned our way and I looked around the room, scanning for the man I saw in the dark shadows of the cellar.

Boris detached himself from the bar. 'Whatever is it, Felicity? Is everything all right?'

I didn't answer him. In fact, I took a pace to my left so I could see around him to the occupants in the room. Before I could say it, Mindy got there first.

'None of the men are wearing a suit and none of them look to have got their hair wet recently.'

Ellis concurred, then added, 'We need to check the rooms.'

He turned to dash from the room. With a nod from me, Mindy went with him. So too the delivery driver whose name I felt I really ought to learn soon. He was mucking in and trying to help. The celebs came to a collective decision that this was not a celebrity activity and stayed behind, filtering into the ballroom as I backed towards the doors again.

'Can you have Buster for a few minutes, please?' I asked Boris. Not waiting for an answer, I crouched to pat Buster on his big, flat skull. 'Stay here in the bar. There's a good dog.'

'*Yup, stay in the bar. Anyone got a bag of pork scratching they want to share?*' he asked, sauntering off toward a table of guests as I went after Mindy.

My day was beginning to feel like a physical test. I was going up and down far too many flights of stairs, and generally running everywhere as if in a blind state of panic. It wasn't panic though; I hadn't had time to stop and think for long enough for panic to set in.

What we had was a small and dwindling window in which to catch the man I'd seen, and I felt an urgent need to find out who it was.

With Ellis leading the way, finding the bedrooms where guests were staying was easy. Without him, I would have needed a map, a compass, possibly a sextant, and probably would have still got lost.

It hadn't occurred to me to check who was in the ballroom so that I would then know who wasn't and thus whose rooms we needed to now visit, but Ellis had. There were seven rooms with people staying in who had elected to watch TV in private or were either happier, or simply felt safer locked inside their suites.

The first was another celebrity couple. Mindy squealed quietly with excitement when the door swung open to reveal a handsome man. His shirt was unbuttoned farther than it needed to be, showing off a well-defined chest. He shot a smile at the four of us gathered outside his door.

'Hey, have you caught the killer?' he asked.

'That's Bruce Force,' squeaked Mindy standing a few inches from me.

Bruce heard her and gave her a smile that made her pant. The delivery man frowned.

I knew Bruce's name because I'd handled the invitations. Like many celebrity weddings, the guest list wasn't about who you were friends with, it was about who you wanted to be seen with. Bruce and his ridiculously pretty girlfriend, Lara Huntsman-Digby were English actors with humble roots just breaking it big in Hollywood. They were darlings of the press currently because of their rags to riches story.

While muscular, Bruce's impressive shoulders were not the ones I'd seen running from the cellar. My brain kept trying to tell me there was something familiar with the silhouette I'd glimpsed. I suspected it was just my mind playing tricks on me and certainly couldn't figure out who it might be if indeed I had seen the man here earlier today.

'It's not him,' I let my team know.

Bruce made a quizzical 'O' with his mouth. 'Who's not who?'

'Have you by any chance seen a large man in a suit who looked drenched?' I asked him.

The quizzical 'O' was joined by a pair of question-filled eyebrows.

Mindy tried to speak but it came out as a squeak. She coughed, and with a red face, tried again. 'Sorry, Bruce. We, um … What I mean is …'

The poor girl couldn't get her mouth to work right. She was staring at the handsome hunk. He was an attractive man, but in his mid-twenties, and thus three decades younger than me, he looked more like a boy to me.

Unlike Vince, echoed an unwelcome voice in my head.

Picking up where my niece left off, I said, 'We are looking for someone in a suit. He ran outside in the storm and we are guessing he is now trying to get into some dry clothes.'

Bruce shrugged. 'Sorry. I've been in here with Lara since we all got together in the ballroom earlier.'

'Lucky girl,' murmured Mindy, her eyes never leaving Bruce's face.

Bruce heard her, tipping her a quick wink. 'You can join us if you like. I can check with Lara, but I'm sure she's up for it.'

My eyes flaring with shock, I grabbed Mindy's arm and started to drag her away. I didn't know how she might respond to such an invitation and had no desire to find out.

'Thank you, Mr Force, we really must be getting along.'

Her feet dragging along the carpet as she let me take her away from temptation, Mindy didn't resist, but equally, she didn't exactly scoff at the idea of joining him.

'You are gorgeous, by the way,' she called as he leaned against his doorframe, smiling his killer smile.

The delivery driver continued to scowl.

I rounded the next corner, having no idea if I was even going the right way or not, but glad to get my niece out of Bruce's captivating sight.

Ellis, looking a little embarrassed after Bruce's indecent proposal, hitched a thumb along the corridor. 'There's another room to check along here.'

The next four rooms proved to be equally disappointing as the persons inside were also clearly not the man I'd seen.

Approaching the sixth, with a jolt I realised I knew who would be in it.

'This is going to be Emma Banks and that awful fiancé of hers, isn't it?'

Ellis nodded.

Mindy screwed up her face. 'He wasn't very nice. What on earth does she see in him?'

'He's rich,' I said with a sigh. 'Harold Cambridge is an internet entrepreneur worth well over eight figures. She just got divorced and even though she took Geoffrey to the cleaners, I know she still lost a good portion of what she had.'

'Yeah, what's with that?' asked Mindy. 'How is she here at his wedding? Surely the two of them should hate each other. Or one should hate the other, at least. That's how the papers made it look.'

I could only shrug my shoulders. 'You saw them earlier in the ballroom. When Harold tried to force Emma to go with him, it was Geoffrey who gave her comfort. Maybe the divorce was a necessary evil and the press made it out to be more emotional than it was.'

Ellis knocked on their door, stepping back so as not to crowd whoever came to answer it. I wanted it to be Emma, because I was going to invite her outside and then quiz her about what Harold had been doing over the last couple of hours without telling her why.

He was one of the men who matched the outline and was roughly the right age for the image in my head. I still couldn't shift the idea that the man I saw had grey hair. Harold's wasn't grey, but it was greying around the sides to give him that salt and pepper look many middle-aged men get in their forties.

When no one came to the door, Ellis knocked again.

After a minute, it became obvious no one was in.

'Do we open it?' asked the delivery driver.

I turned to face him. 'I'm sorry, it's been really remiss of me. I haven't learned your name yet.'

'Kevin,' he replied with a smile. 'It's Kevin um Masters.'

'Kevin um Masters?' repeated Mindy with a giggle. 'It's like you don't know your own name.'

Kevin's face flushed, the poor young man embarrassed by the pretty teenager.

Before he felt a need to fumble for any more words, I said, 'Yes, Ellis. If you can, please open the door.'

He did so, producing a master key from a trouser pocket. He called out as he went in, apologising for the intrusion but there was no one there. Both Emma and Harold were elsewhere.

I was glad in a way. Waiting for them to answer the door and getting no answer, my overactive imagination conjured images of them both lying dead on the bed – the killer's third and fourth victims. Thankfully, that was not the case.

The room looked as any other in the house might. They had unpacked their clothes, put their cosmetics et cetera on the sideboard and made themselves comfortable. It was tidy, but they were not here.

I told Mindy and Kevin to wait by the door and had a swift poke around. I was looking for a wet suit, but I didn't find one.

Harold wasn't the man I'd seen either. Perplexed, frustrated, and getting cold, I needed a break.

'I'm going to go get myself clean, Ellis,' I told him. 'I'll meet you downstairs in a while. I'll let you know if DS Khan calls back.'

'Sure. I'm going to check on the cars,' he replied.

I'd all but forgotten about that. I still wanted to know if we had a car left over and whether that would then lead us to find the identity of the mystery man. I felt sure DS Khan would be able to identify the owner from a registration number if we gave him one.

Ellis locked up Harold and Emma's room once we were back outside and we went in different directions. Mindy came with me and Kevin followed the house manager back to the ballroom where most other people were already gathered.

Heading for a shower and a change of clothes, I had no idea of the surprise in store for me.

Unexpected Late Arrival

Opening my door, I was pleased and relieved to find Amber sitting on my bed.

'Hello, Amber,' I gushed happily, sweeping across the room to pick her up for a fuss.

She took one look at me and darted away.

'*You smell like dirt,*' she hissed at me. '*Go away. You can adore me when you are clean. Mindy can do the adoring for now.*'

I scowled at my cat.

She scowled back. '*Well? Go on. Tell Mindy to get on with the adoring. What's the use of being this attractive and pleasing to be around if nobody strokes my fur and feeds me treats?*'

'Is she saying something?' asked Mindy, coming around me as she made her way to the door that linked our rooms.

I shucked my jacket, holding it up to inspect before accepting, with a sigh, that it was unlikely to ever be clean enough to wear again. I threw it in to the corner by the trash bin.

'Amber thinks you should pet her.'

'*Adore me. Not pet me!*' Amber snapped. '*Petting me sounds so … juvenile. Like something you might do for a dog if you were poor and lonely and not refined enough to keep a cat.*'

Mindy liked the cat so was happy enough to sit on my bed and stroke Amber's fur. Suitably placated, Amber began to purr.

'Did you find the cat you went looking for?' I asked as I kicked off my shoes. I was heading for the bathroom to shed the rest of my clothes since my niece was in my room, but paused with the bathroom door open a crack to hear if Amber had anything to tell me.

'*Oh, yes,*' said Amber, her eyes closed as she luxuriated in having Mindy stroke under her chin.

No other information was forthcoming, but just as I was about to prompt my cat into revealing what she might have learned, Mindy abruptly stopped stroking the cat and stood up.

Amber fell over, crashing into the spot where Mindy had been sat as my niece started in my direction. She had a mean look on her face, one that made me think she was about to hit me.

'Mindy?' I enquired, unsure what was happening and getting worried as she closed the distance to me with fast strides.

She brought a hand up suddenly and I flinched away, my brain insisting she was about to punch me, but she grabbed my face instead, placing a hand over my mouth and another around the back of my head so I couldn't duck away.

Quietly, and with her mouth right next to my ear, she said, 'Shhhh. There's someone in your shower.'

Until that moment I hadn't noticed the sound of the running water coming around the crack of the door as I held it almost closed. It was obvious now though. Steam was escaping too.

There was someone in my shower! And it had to be the man I chased from the cellar. The killer hadn't been found anywhere else because he was hiding in my room!

Mindy exhaled, closing her eyes for a second as she let go of my head and gently pushed me to one side. Then, with both hands, she grabbed her hair and pulled it into a ponytail. A band magically appeared from somewhere to hold it in place, and she unzipped her sports jacket, discarding it on the floor as she cracked her neck one way and then the other.

'Mindy,' I hissed. 'I'll call for help. I'll get a couple of men up here.'

Her head shot around. 'Men? What would I need them for? Tell them to bring a med pack. I'm about to do some damage.'

Before I could say another word, or even think to rush across the room to get my handbag for my phone, Mindy kicked the bathroom door savagely and dived into the mist inside.

I went after her, wafting at the clouds of steam with both hands. I heard an, 'Ooof!' noise of outrushing air. Then Mindy screeched, a nonsensical sound that would be quite at home in a ninja movie and something bulky and heavy flew through the air in front of my face.

It hit the tile and rolled, going out through the bathroom door and back into the main part of my suite.

My disbelieving eyes caught sight of something I had not expected to see when I got out of bed this morning. Something, in fact, that I hadn't seen since my husband, Archie, died three years ago.

I felt my face flush as the tumbling limbs managed to sort themselves out. The man (definitely a man) righted himself and bounced back to his feet to face his aggressor just as Mindy zipped through the door.

Momentarily blinded by the steam, her kick was already aiming at the man's head before she realised who it was. Too late to correct it now, her foot was going to smack the smile right off his face.

Until he stepped back, adjusted his stance, and deflected her blow like a practiced martial arts expert.

Mindy pirouetted away, landing in a crouch from which I knew she could rise and attack again if she wanted.

That wasn't going to happen though because her face was as bright red as mine now. In fact, the only person whose face wasn't bright red was the naked man with his meat and two veg on display.

'Hello, Felicity,' he laughed, fixing me with his shark infested grin.

My hands found their way to either side of my face. 'Vince. What on Earth are you doing here?'

He shot me a confused look. 'You invited me.'

Mindy got up off the carpet. 'Um, I think I should maybe leave you two alone. Next time, Auntie, maybe tell me when you have a boyfriend coming to stay,' she chastised me.

'What? Vince isn't my boyfriend,' I protested. Swinging my face back in his direction, anger creasing my brow, I added, 'And I most certainly didn't invite you.'

'Yes, you did,' he argued.

'Um, I'm going to go,' Mindy tried to back away, pointing both thumbs at the door through to her room, then giving me a double thumbs up. 'Ah, you enjoy the not-boyfriend thing. I really don't need to know the details. Casual shag ... whatever. We're all adults.'

'Arrrrg!' I raged. 'I am not sleeping with him. Nor have I ever, and I do not intend to. Stay right there Mindy, I do not wish to be left alone with this … pest,' I said after dismissing about twenty other words I could have used to describe him.

I got a chuckle from Vince. And here's the thing about when a naked man chuckles – it makes things jiggle. It made me wish he were fat because then it might be the fat jiggling and not something else.

'Can you cover yourself up?' I snapped.

'Why?' he chuckled. 'I've seen you naked. Now you get to see me. It was always going to happen sooner or later.'

'He's seen you naked?' questioned Mindy, her eyes also glued to the jiggling things. 'I thought you said …'

'He let himself into my house,' I growled, not intending to snap at my niece. 'He saw me topless, not naked.'

Vince shrugged. 'Potato patato. You have very nice boobies.'

I didn't think the heat in my face could get any more intense, but it did. Taking a step back, I jutted out an arm, pointing at the bathroom. 'Get back in there and find something to wear.'

'My clothes are in the wardrobe. I unpacked already.'

I shook my head. It was one disturbing revelation after another. 'What do you mean your clothes are in my wardrobe? Why on earth would you do that?'

He frowned at me. 'Because you invited me down here. I figured that was your way of saying …'

'I did not invite you,' I growled through gritted teeth. I turned to ask Mindy to help me get rid of the man and his clothes, but she had already fled. The door between our rooms closed before I could say anything and locked with a resounding turn of a key.

Vince went to the bathroom, snagged a towel, and returned. He was using it to dry his hair and body, not cover himself up, and he was talking while he was doing it.

'You told me all about how you were coming down to this posh celebrity wedding here this weekend. Why would you do that if you didn't want me to know exactly where to find you?'

'And you think that was an invitation?

He shrugged. 'I thought you were being deliberately coy.'

My teeth were clamped together like my jaw was wired shut, but I managed to say, 'I was being conversational. Nothing else.'

He shrugged again. 'My mistake. We are here though ...'

'Get. Out!' I shouted, jerking a straight arm toward the door.

'As I am?'

'Yes!' I re-emphasised my point by folding my arm in and jerking it at the door again.

He shrugged but didn't argue. 'Okay.'

He rubbed his hair with the towel, then flicked it lazily over one shoulder as he padded barefoot and naked to my door.

He opened it with everything still on show.

Ellis Carter blasphemed loudly in shock. He was standing outside my door with his hand raised to knock on it.

Vince turned around. 'There's someone here to see you.'

I am not prone to violence but had there been something blunt and heavy to hand, I am certain I would have thrown it at the naked man in my doorway. I knew just where I wanted to aim.

Ellis's eyes were about as wide as they could get, and his mouth was hanging open as he fought for something to say.

Feeling ready to kill, I harrumphed loudly and started yelling. 'Get back in my bathroom and take some clothes with you. Do not come out until you are dressed!'

Vince folded his arms and stared at me. The sideways, dangerous smile was back.

'So now you want me to stay?'

In my head I was throttling him, I swear. My right eye twitched and he took it as an unspoken cue to stop annoying me. With a chuckle, he tied the towel around his waist and went to my wardrobe. He wasn't lying when he said he'd unpacked. There were suits and shirts on the hangers inside.

Turning my attention to Ellis, I flicked my eyebrows to ask him why he was at my door.

Vince started whistling a merry tune to himself as he selected garments to wear.

Still looking like he wanted to escape, Ellis mumbled, 'Um, there is a car without an owner.'

The search for the identity of the mystery man was getting somewhere, but the instant a ray of hope blossomed, my brain stomped on it.

'It's a big SUV, isn't it?'

Ellis's expression changed, confusion settling onto his brow. 'Yes. How did you know that?'

Vince was across the room now, fishing around in the drawer where I had placed my underwear. I was about to yell at him again when he fished out a pair of what were obviously his shorts and then a pair of socks.

I was snarling with rage when I refocused my eyes on Ellis to answer his question.

'Because it's his car,' I growled, making it clear with my eyes I was talking about the male intruder in my room. He was at least, finally donning some underwear. 'That was you in the cellar too, wasn't it?'

Vince looked up from putting on his socks. 'Yes, dear.'

'Don't call me dear,' I warned him through teeth I was clenching so hard I thought I might be about to chip them.

'You've been following me around since you got here, haven't you?' I demanded to know. I was putting two and two together – that feeling I had of being watched was because Vince had been lurking just out of sight.

He slipped his arms into his shirt. 'I arrived to the sound of a scream. People were running around and getting excited. I thought it would be best if I stayed in the shadows and did what I do best.'

'Irritate people?' I guessed.

He sniggered at me like I'd made a big joke. 'No, silly.' He turned his attention to the man standing in my doorway. 'I'm Vince Slater, a licenced private investigator and security expert.'

Ellis shook Vince's hand though he still looked as though he wanted to run away and come back later. Or never. It was hard to tell what people felt around Vince.

Vince continued to explain himself as he flicked his trousers and started to put them on.

'Hearing there was a dead body, I decided to start snooping.'

'Wait a second?' I held up a hand to stop him talking. 'Where were you? When I was in the honeymoon suite talking to the grooms and Quentin's body was lying on the carpet, where were you?'

'In a room across the hall,' Vince admitted. 'I had the door open a crack so I could see and hear.'

'All the rooms are locked, sir,' argued Ellis.

Vince just smiled at him – I already knew Vince knew how to defeat a lock. It also explained how someone got into the cellar. I had been meaning to ask Ellis about where else we could put the body, but now I suspected there was no need.

Threading on his belt, Vince said, 'I've been poking around and listening to conversations for the last couple of hours. The police are unlikely to get here, and you have two murders already. Someone in this house is a killer and I'm not convinced they are going to stop at two.'

'Why ever not?' begged Ellis, horrified at the thought.

Vince zipped his trousers and gave himself a pat, wiggling his hips as if he were making sure everything was in place. Men are so weird.

'Why two murders?' he asked. 'One I can understand. The first one, assuming Quentin was the first to die and not just the first to be found, had to be deliberate. A person sets out to kill someone and believes they either have a reason or they have no choice ... whatever the motivations behind it, they choose to kill. However, it would appear the second man is yet to be identified, is that right?'

'Yes,' agreed Ellis, still hovering just outside my door.

'So no one here knows him. I took a copy of his fingerprints ...'

'So that's what you were doing?' I nodded my head, finally working out why the mystery body had ink on his fingertips.

'Yes, dear,' replied Vince, flicking a tie around his neck. 'I should have an answer in a little while. That is if the poor chap is on a police database anywhere. I have a few friends in the police,' he explained idly as he stared down his chest to figure out which bit of his tie needed to go where.

'But how did he get here?' asked Ellis. 'If the SUV belongs to this gentleman, and we can assume he didn't travel with anyone else because no one recognises him, then ...'

'No one admits to recognising him,' Vince corrected Ellis's statement. 'That, in my line of work, is an important distinction.'

I scrunched up my face as I tried to make his suggestion fit. 'But that would mean ... there would have to be a conspiracy.'

'Perhaps,' Vince agreed, giving one end of his tie a yank, and turning to the mirror to make sure it was right. 'Now that I am … out in the open, shall we say. I can bring my full deductive capabilities to bear.'

My face scrunched up a little more. 'Hold on. This is my case.'

I got a raised eyebrow in response.

'You're a wedding planner, darling,' he reminded me with a gentle smile.

I threw a pillow at his face. It was all I had to hand.

'Nevertheless, Vincent, I am going to work out who killed Quentin. I will figure out who the mystery body is, and I will be the one to present the police with a killer when they get here.' I want to claim that I don't know what came over me, but truthfully, I did. Vince had this unmatched ability to rub me up the wrong way. He got under my skin and made me want to tear my eyeballs out.

If he'd politely offered to take over, I probably would have thanked him and wished him luck, but he didn't. Instead, he belittled me and made it sound like I needed to be rescued by the big brave man. I was borrowing Mindy's attitude – there was work to do and I didn't require a man to get the job done.

His raised eyebrows settled back to their normal positions.

'Righty then. I guess I'll be in the bar if you need me,' he started toward the door. 'Come along, Ellis, I think the lady probably wants to get cleaned up.'

I really did.

Vince went out the door, pulling it shut behind him and I began to unbutton my dress.

Vince shot his head back through the narrow gap.

'I can stick around if you want a hand getting clean,' he offered.

The bedside lamp smashed against the doorframe a half second after the door shut again and half an inch from where his stupid smile had been.

Humans are Boring

I was feeling calmer by the time I got out of the shower. I was clean at least, though I washed my hair twice to be certain all the rat poop was out of it.

Amber looked my way when I peered around the bathroom door to make sure Vince wasn't in my suite somewhere. I half expected to find him lying in my bed with a red rose between his teeth.

Seeing Amber on my bed instead of Vince prompted two questions. The first was less important than the second, but got top billing, nevertheless.

'Did it not occur to you to tell me there was a man in my shower?'

Amber blinked. Once, slowly and deliberately. It felt like the cat version of a deliberate yawn to show I was boring her.

'*I assumed you knew,*' she replied in a disinterested way. '*He is your mate, after all.*'

The twitch in my right eye was back. 'He is not my mate. Why does everyone – even my pets – think that?'

'*Because of how you are together,*' Amber argued. '*You both keep taking off your removeable pelts and there is all this ... passion whenever you are together.*'

'Passion is not a word I would use.'

'*Well, that's what it sounds and looks like.*'

Sensing that I was losing an argument to a cat, I switched topics to ask my second question. It was one I'd asked before.

'What did you learn from the cats?'

Amber stretched out a back leg and started grooming it. *'The cat who was in the room saw men fighting. That is why she was hiding under the bed. She had been on top of it asleep until the humans began to struggle with each other.'*

Having thrown down the gauntlet at Vince, I wanted desperately to be able to solve the mystery and catch the killer. I even had a secret ninja sidekick in Mindy if I needed someone to restrain the killer once I identified who it was.

To say I was keen to hear what Amber had to say would be a massive understatement.

'Go on,' I begged. 'Who was it?'

Amber tilted her head to one side, giving me a curious look. *'It was another man.'*

'A man?'

'Yes. Man or men. Might have been a woman. Hard to tell really.'

'Hard to tell?' I shook my head in disbelief. 'You must be able to narrow it down better than that.'

'Humans all look and smell roughly the same to a cat. We can tell the difference between male and female and young and old. As a race you are just not interesting enough for us to remember more detail than that.' She went back to licking her leg.

I closed my eyes and gave myself a five count as I waited for the tic by my right eye to stop twitching.

'Amber, dear,' I cooed, causing the cat to look up again. 'Bringing me the description that it was a human does not get you a poached mackerel.'

'*Poached in milk,*' she reminded me.

'I need to know which of the people staying in this house the other cat saw in the room with Quentin.'

'*Quentin is the dead one?*' she tried to confirm.

'Yes. Can you get the other cat to identify who it was? Perhaps she could claw a leg for me or climb onto a lap. Anything that makes it obvious which one she saw. Did she say that she saw Quentin being killed?'

'*No. She was hiding under the bed.*'

'Did she hear their conversation? Maybe something was said that would tell me why he chose to murder my friend.'

Amber stopped grooming herself and stood up, stretching her front legs out and then her back ones as she limbered up.

'*I will ask, but human conversation is even more boring than your faces. I doubt she will remember anything.*' Amber jumped down from the bed and vanished through the fireplace again.

With a sigh, I started dressing.

Mindy

On my way back to the bar, I knocked for Mindy. She was in her room practicing yoga and still wasn't wearing wedding planner appropriate attire. I had changed into a floral dress with matching hand-stitched heels. A dusty pink jacket complimented the outfit perfectly as did the handbag I'd chosen. Trust me, when you dress for weddings almost every day of your life, you find yourself with an extensive wardrobe of suitable outfits.

Mindy had changed – probably because she got damp yanking Vince from my shower – but her new clothes were little different from the previous ones.

'Tomorrow, you need to be suitably dressed, Mindy,' I insisted.

'Of course, Auntie. I would have put something nice on now, but we still have a killer to catch, don't we?'

'We do,' I lamented with a sigh. We had a killer to catch because when the chance to shake off the task came, I dug my heels in and held on to it. I am such an idiot.

She shrugged. 'I might need to hand him his teeth. Figure of speech, Auntie,' she added quickly when she saw my horrified face. 'The dresses I have aren't much good for that.'

I remembered her hitching her skirt up to kick a policeman in the face a week ago. The man had been so shocked at the teenager running at him with her knickers on display, he'd failed to defend himself at all.

I might not like what she was wearing – it failed to set the right tone – but she made a fair point about its practicality, and I wasn't going to argue.

The hallways of the house were quiet, no footsteps and no voices as we walked along them. Mindy made no noise at all, her running shoes silent on the carpet. The only sound, other than the storm howling outside, was the click click of my heels.

The sky, which had been dark before due to the heavy clouds outside, was now black as afternoon gave way to evening.

Just as we got back to the ballroom, and the hubbub of conversation coming from it, my phone rang. Taking it from my handbag, it wasn't a number I recognised, so when I answered it, I said, 'Felicity Philips, professional wedding planner to the stars. How may I help you?'

'Mrs Philips, this is DS Khan. I'm afraid there is no way for me to get to you yet. The coast guard have already launched their rescue craft to help a yacht in trouble out in the Channel. However, they were adamant they wouldn't be able to dock at the island to let me off even if their boat came back in. I will be with you as soon as the storm begins to dissipate. Has there been any development?'

Buster spotted me as we came through the doors and was hustling over to greet me, his back end wobbling from side to side as he wagged his tail.

He stopped when he got to me. *'Ewww, you smell of cat. Did Amber return? I felt for sure she would get lost or eaten or something.'*

Mindy scooped him for a hug, nuzzling his neck with her face, while also proving how much stronger than me she was. I could only just about lift Buster.

To the detective sergeant, I said, 'Not yet. No one else is dead if that is what you are asking. Not that I know of, anyway.'

'Okay, Mrs Philips. Please just sit tight, tell people to stay in their rooms or congregate somewhere they feel safe, and we will be there as soon as the storm allows it.'

I let him go, looking around the bar as I slipped my phone away. I knew everyone in the bar by name because it was my job to be so well informed. However, I could count on one hand the number of people I actually knew.

Vince was sitting at the bar with his back to me. It made him look like he was sulking though such behaviour felt out of character for the well-dressed pirate. A small voice at the back of my head reminded me that I liked how he looked in his suits and could now add that he looked just as good out of them.

I refused to listen to what the voice had to say.

Geoffrey and Anton both put down their drinks and came across to speak with me as I made my way through the room.

Anton started speaking first, 'We felt we needed to thank you for sorting out our room.'

'How is it?' I enquired.

'It is every bit as good as the room we were in,' replied Geoffrey. He was being generous, but they knew I could do no better than I already had.

'Yes,' agreed Anton. 'Every bit as good. You really are going above and beyond for us, Felicity.'

I dipped my head in thanks. 'That is what I promise for all my clients.'

'Well, look, we've recovered from the shock,' Anton took over, speaking for both he and his partner. 'And we wanted to muck in and help.'

'Help?' I wasn't sure what they were suggesting.

'With the investigation,' Geoffrey explained. 'We all know there is a killer among us or hiding somewhere in the house. This is supposed to be our wedding weekend, but instead of relaxing, all of our guests are tense.'

'They are all looking about at each other as if trying to work out if the person across from them killed two people,' added Anton. 'We thought that if we got everyone to chip in, we might be able to find ... evidence,' he suggested weakly.

'We heard you chased a man in the cellar,' said Geoffrey, hopefully.

A small snort of amusement forced its way past my lips. 'I found out who it was. That was not the killer. That was a ... friend of mine.' I chose to refer to Vince as a friend because using the term I had reserved for him in my head would make the wax run from my clients' ears.

'Oh,' Geoffrey looked disappointed. 'Well, we heard there was a car no one could account for.'

'It belongs to the same friend.'

Anton and Geoffrey were starting to look crestfallen.

'Could we get some of our friends and guests to help look for the camera and laptop?' enquired Anton tentatively as if he expected me to knock him back again.

I almost told him there was no need, but forming a posse to search the house, this time with the grooms convincing everyone to play along, sounded like a good move. Especially if they did find something. Besides, I didn't really have a next step to take.

'That sounds like a great idea,' I beamed at my happy couple.

Energised by the chance to do something, my grooms spun about and began speaking loudly to the room. They asked for everyone's help, and to my surprise people were instantly getting to their feet. Perhaps they were bored just sitting around. Those who were less inclined to join in soon found themselves in the minority.

'Dinner will be served at seven,' called Boris. 'Can everyone please return to the ballroom in time for it?'

He got thankful replies from hungry people who were being sorted into groups. No one wanted to wander the old house alone or paired up with a person they didn't know so they were forming trios and quads to explore.

Anton and Geoffrey – who had once played a police chief inspector in a TV show – were leading everyone, and it had the feeling of a parlour game one might have seen played in Victorian England. They were all off to hunt for missing items like it was a scavenger hunt.

As the bar emptied, those who were not playing along became easier to spot. Vince was still sitting at the bar though he was watching me now, a smile teasing the corners of his eyes.

Harold hadn't moved either. I hadn't noticed he was in the bar until now; the press of people had hidden him. Sitting at a table by himself, he was working, a laptop demanding his attention.

He hadn't been shown the photograph yet.

I walked across to him, Buster trotting along by my feet.

'Mr Cambridge, I need to show you a photograph,' I announced, signalling for Mindy to bring her phone.

'I'm busy,' he dismissed me without even looking up.

Patiently, I tried again. 'Too busy to look at one photograph? I'm sure you can spare me the time for that.'

He swore under his breath, happily displaying a lack of manners, patience, and decorum.

Boris heard him. 'Sir, I shall ask you to hold your tongue. There are ladies present.'

Harold got to his feet, towering over me and Boris, his desire to threaten and intimidate quite clear. I smiled up at him, but his attention was on Boris now.

'What are you gonna do about it?' he growled, narrowing his eyes at the shorter, older man.

Mindy stepped in with her camera. 'Do you recognise this man?' she asked, quite deliberately trying to defuse the situation.

Vince was watching from the bar. I couldn't say what was going on in Harold's head; he'd been acting surly since the first time I saw him, but I knew if he chose to get physical, Vince would step in, so I stared up at the aggressive multi-millionaire and held my smile.

'This is the second victim,' I explained. 'No one seems to know who he is.'

However, being pleasant and polite to him did nothing to alter his mood. 'Get that phone out of my face,' he snapped, attempting a backhand swipe to push Mindy's arm away.

It was a mistake.

My niece caught his wrist with her free hand, deftly applied pressure as she twisted it inward and stepped to her right as she manoeuvred Harold's shoulder. I've seen such things done before on television but never up close. She looked as if her heartrate hadn't even changed.

Buster barked, *'Let's get him!'* darting forward to bite a leg. I had to grab him quickly, ducking down to get hold of his back legs. The daft dog continued trying to join in, snapping thin air with his teeth as I pulled him away on his belly. *'Let me at him!'*

I got clear as Harold found himself forced downward. He was screaming blue murder, threatening violent retribution, and using words a lady ought to never hear.

Behind us, people had been filtering out of the bar to start searching the house, but every last one of them reversed course to find out what all the noise was.

'I do not like violent men,' said Mindy, calmly.

Harold replied with a torrent of curse words. She was still only using one hand, the other held her phone which she placed in front of his face on the table.

'Do you recognise this man?' Mindy asked.

Again, she got an unprintable response. It was followed by a squeal of pain as Mindy applied a little more pressure to Harold's wrist.

'Arrrgh! You're going to break my arm!'

Mindy shook her head. 'No, your elbow joint will snap before that happens. Breaking bones can happen, but it is generally the cartilage that gives first. Perhaps you can provide an answer and we can end this before I am forced to do permanent damage.'

I was beginning to worry she might snap his arm just to make a point.

'Mindy perhaps it is time to let him go,' I suggested. 'I am sure he will look at the photograph for us.'

Harold sneered, 'I'm going to sue you all!' Then he squealed again as Mindy applied a fraction more pressure.

Undeterred, Mindy leaned her face down so it was an inch from Harold's ear. 'The picture, please. I don't think a man swinging his arm to hit a teenage woman will do very well when he tries to sue. If you don't look at the photograph, I'll not only snap your arm, I'll report your attempted assault to the police.'

'I think she means it,' I urged Harold to comply.

Finally, Harold caved. 'I don't know him! Okay? I've never seen him before!'

Mindy opened her hand, releasing Harold's arm. She said, 'Thank you,' as she picked up her phone and slid it back into the pouch on the hip of her stretchy pants.

I worried Harold might attack her, but all he could do was slump into his chair and massage his tender arm. He wasn't done talking though.

'I am going to sue you,' he snarled at the back of Mindy's head. 'My lawyers will tear you apart.'

'Really?' scoffed Boris. 'With so many witnesses willing to say you were the aggressive one? Don't be so ridiculous.'

Biting on his words and seething with anger, Harold slammed his laptop closed, hooked it under his good arm and stormed from the room.

It had been an ugly display of temper by a man I suspected capable of violence. Emma had seemed scared of him earlier and as I remembered that previous incident, I found myself frowning. There was a question I suddenly wanted an answer to.

'Has anyone seen Emma?'

Discoveries

No one had an answer to my question. Harold had stormed off, presumably heading for his room, so putting yet more mileage into my day, we trailed back up there after him.

There were people in the hallways now, which made the house feel a little less dangerous and foreboding. With Buster leading the way, even though the daft dog didn't know where he was going, Ellis, Mindy, and I returned to the room assigned to Harold and Emma. Here at the back of the house, we were alone again, listening to the wind howling outside and the occasional crack of thunder as the storm raged outside.

Ellis knocked and waited just as he had not so very long ago.

Buster was sniffing at the base of the door, his snorting/grunting noises echoing in the quiet of the corridor.

No answer came.

Ellis knocked again, repeating the process of waiting and calling out before opening the door with his master key.

Wherever Harold had gone, it wasn't to his room as it was still empty. There was no sign of Emma either. It was all a little frustrating. I had no reason to believe Emma had come to any harm, yet there was an uncomfortable feeling in my gut that wanted to believe the worst.

Buster interrupted my worrying thoughts. *'This smells the same as where we found the body.'*

'You mean Quentin?' I asked him.

'Yes. It's the same floral female human smell.'

I pressed him. 'Exactly the same?'

'Um, Auntie,' Mindy hissed to get my attention.

I looked her way, but my eyes stopped when they got to Ellis Carter. He was eyeing me sceptically. I'd been talking to Buster and doing it openly again. My cheeks coloured.

'I was, um … I like to try to guess what he is saying when he barks like that,' I tried an unconvincing lie.

Ellis skewed his lips to one side but didn't challenge my claim.

Buster continued talking anyway. *'It's definitely the same smell,'* he snorted with his nose in the air.

I tried a little laugh, 'I think he's saying he can smell Emma's perfume.'

Ellis frowned.

Mindy came to my rescue, clapping her hands and saying, 'Back to the bar?'

Being asked a question forced me to answer and thus gave me a reason to avoid Ellis's curious gaze. I'd been having a conversation with my dog and I doubted I was going to convince him that wasn't what he saw.

He locked the door to Harold and Emma's room again and followed us back downstairs.

There, we discovered the wedding guests had already made a discovery.

'They were outside on the lawn,' said Hopster, an attractive young black man doing well in popular music. I couldn't name any of his … I wanted to call them records because that's what they were to me but knew Mindy would call them something else. She could probably tell me all about him, but I was more interested in what he had to say. 'I spotted them through the window,' he told us.

'They were just discarded?' I questioned.

We were looking at a complete change of men's clothing. Shoes, socks, trousers, a shirt, and a waist-length coat. It was all completely soaked; wringing wet, in fact, because it had been outside in the rain.

Hopster spotted them more by accident than anything else, but then went out into the storm to retrieve them.

He was with another man of about the same age and a very pretty young woman. The woman was Hopster's girlfriend, a rising model called Glitzy though her real name was Janet Mayflower. The other man, a pale-skinned Irish chap with bright ginger hair, was Hopster's partner, Graham McMullin, the one doing the music to Hopster's lyrics.

Graham asked, 'Do you think this might be the clothing the second victim was wearing?'

'Why would he take it all off?' asked Glitzy, her picture-perfect face scrunched in confusion.

Hopster stared at her for a second before saying, 'It's a good thing you're pretty.'

His comment drew a smile from her, the veiled insult about her intelligence going straight over her head.

'I think the killer probably stripped him after he killed him,' guessed Graham.

I had to agree. 'But why?' I wanted to know. 'Why kill him in the first place? But also, what did the killer gain by stripping off his clothes?'

No one had an answer for me.

Wedding guests were drifting back to the bar in threes and fours, returning because they were getting hungry, and it was nearly dinner time. The find drew their interest.

Kevin the delivery driver appeared though I didn't think he'd come in with the wedding guests. In fact, I couldn't now remember seeing him in the ballroom when the grooms rallied everyone and set off to search the house. I dismissed it, assuming he must have been visiting a restroom at the time.

'Are they the clothes from the naked mystery man?' he guessed the same as everyone else. 'Where were they?'

'On the lawn outside. I found them,' replied Hopster proudly.

Kevin wasn't interested in the wet clothes. Not really. He chose to join us because he had an eye on Mindy. He was being surreptitious about it, but he couldn't be more than a few years older than her, and my niece is quite pretty. Also, Mindy hadn't been coy about eyeing him up when she got the chance.

'I need to see where you found them,' I announced, pushing away from the crowd gathering to see what we were looking at.

Hopster said, 'Sure. I'll show you.'

'Can we do it without going outside?' I wondered as another crack of thunder seemed to rock the house.

He chuckled at me. 'Sure. We can look out the window. That's how I spotted them.'

Heading for the door, I found a small troop of people following me. It included Buster and Mindy, but also Kevin and Ellis.

We bumped into Boris just as we left the bar.

'Hattie and Eric are no longer here,' I observed. 'Are they likely to return or do anything else to cause alarm or upset?'

'I sent them to their accommodation. I made it sound like they could have the rest of the day off. Say, you don't think they could have something to do with what happened, do you?'

The thought had crossed my mind. They were close by when Quentin was discovered, and it was Hattie who found the second body. I ruled them out earlier when I spotted Vince running from the cellar but was yet to find out who it was. Now though … was homophobia enough to make old people kill?

Unable to pinpoint how I felt about them and the likelihood of their involvement, I said, 'I might need to speak to them later.' Mindy, Ellis, Hopster, and Kevin were waiting at the door for me with Buster. 'We are just going to look where the mystery man's clothing was found.'

'You found it?' Boris sounded surprised.

'I saw it outside the window,' Hopster boasted.

'I'm going to see where it was, just in case that reveals anything.' I didn't think it would but was trying to be thorough.

Boris let us go, settling into a chair near the bar. Watching him, and seeing how weary he looked, my eyes were drawn to where Vince had been sitting earlier. He wasn't there now, and he wasn't off with the wedding guests searching the house. So where was he?

My eye twitched and I raced from the ballroom after Hopster and my merry band of helpers.

The room Hopster took us to wasn't that far away and it wasn't far from where the second body was found. I'd assumed the rap star had been on one of the upper floors looking down when he saw the discarded clothing, but he'd been on the ground floor looking out.

'It was right there, man,' said Hopster standing at the window and pointing out to the darkness.

'How did you even see it?' asked Kevin, raising a good point because I couldn't even see the grass.

A flash of lightning turned the world outside pure white for a split second.

Hopster grinned. 'That's how. The searching thing was boring, so I popped in here for a smoke and spotted the clothes when the lightning lit up the garden.'

I backtracked from the room – an empty storage space that used to house the silverware according to Ellis – and into the corridor outside. The open door Hattie came to close was fifty feet away and we were only twenty feet from the closet where she discovered the body.

'Someone stripped him and threw his clothes outside,' I murmured to myself.

Mindy was standing close enough to hear me. 'But why?' she asked. 'I can understand taking his wallet so we wouldn't know who it was, but why take his clothes off.'

'Maybe he took them off himself,' suggested Kevin. 'Perhaps it was something sexual and ... I dunno, I'm just guessing,' his voice trailed off.

I didn't think the victim was down here engaged in something sordid. I couldn't rule it out, but I thought it more likely there was something else going on. I just had no idea what it was.

'Why kill Quentin?' I asked myself. 'Is it even the same killer?'

Kevin latched on to that instantly. 'Good point,' he said encouragingly. 'Maybe there are two killers here.'

'Felicity, darling,' Vince's annoyingly upbeat voice reached my ears. He was calling out as he made his way in our direction.

Buster barked, *'Here, Vince,'* helpfully. Vince wouldn't understand my dog but could follow the sound of his barking.

Mindy came up to my shoulder. 'What's the deal with you two, Auntie. Are you dating or not?'

'Yes, they are,' said Buster.

'No, we are not,' I replied to Mindy.

'But you did go on a date,' Mindy pointed out.

She had me there. 'I was coerced into that date.' I really was. 'Besides, it wasn't exactly a date. We went for dinner and we never even got to eat.'

'Because you got arrested,' Mindy reminded me.

Vince came into view, rounding a corner to find us waiting for him before I had to give any further thought to the subject.

'They found a camera and laptop,' he announced. 'The laptop is dead, but they think it's just the battery.'

'Really? Where were they?' asked Kevin sounding startled.

Vince looked at the young delivery driver thoughtfully. 'Well, that's an interesting question for you to ask.'

I felt my right eyebrow make its way north. 'Why is it?'

Vince kept his eyes on Kevin. 'Because it was in his delivery van.'

Guilty

Kevin looked like a deer caught in headlights. The confident, helpful attitude was gone, replaced by a fearful, nervous expression as all eyes swung his way.

He took a step backward, away from my accusing glare, but found Buster right behind his ankles.

Kevin tripped and fell, terror showing in his face.

'*Ha!*' growled Buster. '*Dog one, human nil.*' He curled his top lip back to show his teeth and snarled meaningfully.

'Buster, enough,' I commanded. Even I could hear the anger in my voice when I directed my next words at the young man on the floor, 'I think you have some explaining to do.'

Mindy came to stand over Kevin. She wasn't doing anything, but her hands were loose at her sides in case he thought it a good idea to try to run or put up a fight.

He wasn't going to though. There were half a dozen of us in the corridor with him and he was surrounded.

Vince was still twenty feet away, lounging against the wall, but he chose that moment to shove off with his shoulder. 'I think we should take him somewhere private for a little chat.'

Kevin blurted, 'I didn't kill anyone.'

'*I'll be bad cop*,' volunteered Buster in his rasping Devil Dog voice.

Kevin wasn't trying to get up or get away, but he'd been quick to include himself in the investigation when it started. He was the one who came with Mindy and me and was hanging around us. Was that so he knew how we were getting on and could steer what we were doing? I thought about how he'd been surprised when Hopster found the clothes and was ready to suggest the dead mystery man might have been involved in something sexual as an explanation for his nakedness.

Ellis came forward. 'We can use my office.'

By the time we came back to the central hub of the house where the ballroom and bar could be found, word had already spread about the laptop and camera and where they'd been found. Kevin had stashed them inside a bag in the passenger's footwell. It was a deliberate attempt to hide the evidence he knew we were looking for.

There were some questioning stares from the wedding guests as we went by the door to the bar. Kevin's eyes were focused on the carpet – the look of a condemned man on his face. He'd killed two people and done his best to stop us catching him. If it were not for the storm, he would have escaped the island and maybe never have been caught.

Instead, he got trapped here and now he could feel the noose around his own neck. The police would come when they were able and would find the killer in our custody ready to hand over. I felt genuinely jubilant though I knew I couldn't show it.

Ellis led us to the front of the house where his office was located.

'We'll be left alone in here,' he assured me as I went in.

It was a small room with a desk against one wall. There were no other chairs, but as I put my handbag down, Ellis appeared with two. They were small and wooden, and I didn't know where he had got them from, but I thanked him and offered one to Vince.

'Thank you, darling,' Vince winked at me.

The tic in my right eye twitched several times, forcing me to press a finger to my face to make it stop.

Kevin was backed against the wall with Vince, Ellis, Mindy, and me staring at him. Buster was by my feet and he was staring too.

'Who is the naked man we found?' I demanded to know.

Kevin shook his head and tried to shrug. When he spoke, his voice cracked and came out as a squeak. 'I don't know,' he managed on his second attempt. 'I told you already, I didn't do it. I haven't killed anyone.'

'How did the laptop and camera come to be in your van?' Vince wanted to know.

Again, Kevin offered us a helpless expression. 'I have no idea.' Then he clicked his fingers as something came to him. 'I left it unlocked when I was making my deliveries, I always do. I bet someone put it in there then.'

Vince shook his head. 'Try again.'

'You volunteered to be part of our group,' I pointed out. 'Right from the start, you wanted to be involved.'

'I was … I was just trying to help out,' he stuttered. 'I'm stuck here like everyone else, and I have nothing better to do. I don't know anyone so I figured I would muck in. It's not like I was going to fit in with all the celebrities.'

I nodded at his response but said, 'You see, I think the reason you offered to help is because you wanted to make sure we didn't find evidence that might lead us in your direction. I think you were helping out so you could keep an eye on us.'

'That's just not true,' he argued weakly. 'You have to believe me. I don't know either of the men who have been killed. I came here to deliver food for the party.'

We prodded and probed him for a few more minutes, getting nowhere, and I was beginning to wonder if he was telling the truth. Stopping Vince from asking whatever question he had lined up next, I pulled him and the others to one side.

'Should we have a look at the laptop? Maybe they got it working already.' I suggested.

Vince sniffed, drawing in a deep breath as he thought. 'We don't have anything on him. Finding the laptop and camera in his car proves nothing. He could easily be telling the truth.'

'We're not going to just let him go, are we?' asked Mindy, making it clear she thought that would be a terrible idea.

I turned to Ellis. 'Have you got anywhere we can put him?'

The house manager raised his eyebrows. 'You mean like somewhere we can lock him up? No, not that I can think of. I mean, we could lock him in a bedroom, I suppose, but there would be nothing to stop him going out of the window.'

Vince shook his head. 'We can tie him up and keep him in the bar where he can be seen. I am right in thinking the photographer was here alone?'

I said, 'Yes,' wondering why he was asking.

'Then we can assume no one is going to take retribution,' Vince concluded.

'I stole them,' said Kevin, shame dripping from his voice.

We all turned to face him.

Kevin's eyes were locked on the carpet. 'I'm sorry,' he snivelled, barely able to keep the tears from falling. 'They were just there on the desk in his room. He was outside taking photographs when I arrived. He said the storm was too spectacular to miss so he was taking pictures while it was still in the distance. We chatted for a bit – I'm into photography, but I have to do it on my phone, I can't afford all the fancy gear he's got. When I heard he had killed himself, I snuck up to his room, I knew which one was his because it's at the back of the house and I saw him up there earlier on the balcony. It was just before I finished unloading.' Kevin let go a deep sigh, his shoulders dropping as he deflated. 'I went to his room and snatched the items I knew I could never afford. Being a delivery driver doesn't pay much.'

No one spoke for a few seconds, and Kevin twitched his eyes up to see if we were looking at him. He dropped them back to the carpet when he saw the judgement on our faces.

'So you're a thief but not a murderer?' I asked him to confirm.

'I'll be no trouble,' he promised. 'You don't have to tie me up. I'll even continue to help look for the killer if you'll let me.' He looked up again, meeting my gaze with hopeful eyes.

'I don't think so.' I said the words with almost no emotion behind them. I felt like a disappointed parent. Dismissing him, I turned to Ellis, 'I think we need to keep him somewhere public as Vince suggests. The police can talk to him when they arrive.'

Admitting he'd stolen Quentin's things was probably going to cost Kevin his job. I would report his dishonesty to Barry, my chief catering supplier, in the morning. What Barry chose to do would be up to him, but I would not be happy to have the young thief supplying any of my events again. However, owning up to being a thief gave us a reason for the laptop and camera to be in his van. I didn't know how much of his story was true, but I believed he was more likely to be an opportunist thief than a homicidal maniac.

I was disappointed, that was the chief emotion I felt on my way back to the bar area. For a brief moment I thought I had caught a killer. Had I done so, we could have put the weekend back on track. Instead, whoever did kill Quentin was still at large, still on this island, and still potentially very dangerous.

From ground level, Buster made a snuffling snorted noise. He did it a lot, and I learned to ignore it long ago, so I hardly even noticed it now. Vince however cocked an eyebrow.

'Is he all right?'

'*I can smell blood,*' announced my dog.

I almost blurted out a question in response, only just managing to catch myself before I did. We were just about to reach the doors to the ballroom and bar where people were starting to get their dinner, when Ian Riggs, the reality TV singing star came hurtling around the corner and into the corridor ahead of us. He had blood on his hands and on his shirt and a panicked look on his face.

'Help!' he shouted, screeching to a stop on the carpet five yards away. He was already starting to backpeddle. 'Someone's been attacked! I found blood on the banister. It's fresh!' he lifted his hands to show us.

A heartbeat later I was running.

Faint

I stopped a few yards later to kick off my impractical heels but had already been left behind by the younger and fitter people. Only Vince hung on for me though I was sure he could have left me in his dust too, had he chosen to do so.

Kevin ran alongside Mindy, and I let him go. He was a thief by his own admission, but not a killer and I believed him. Nevertheless, I wanted to put him in a corner of the bar where he could be watched, but that was going to have to wait as we raced through the hallways to find the latest drama.

Ian's shout had been loud enough to reach the people in the bar and ballroom, and urgent enough to get them moving. Feet thundered past me, a crowd of wedding guests all jostling in the hallways as they fought to catch up with those ahead.

Even in the vast house, it was easy to follow the noise of those in front to arrive at the latest scene of carnage.

My heart was in my throat, worry making my stomach do flip flops as the air in my lungs began to sear from the effort of running.

Buster was wheezing along at my side and I was using his slow pace as an excuse for my own.

'He's not really built for running,' I gasped at Vince, convincingly out of breath myself.

Buster puffed and panted, *'Devil Dog needs a mode of transport. Something black so it merges with the shadows.'*

Vince looked at the wedding guests shooting off ahead of us. Mindy had already disappeared from sight. Reaching a decision, Vince scooped

Buster, tucking him under his right arm like a rugby ball as he started running again.

'*This is much better,*' sighed my dog, his tongue lolling from his mouth by almost a foot.

So much for using his glacial pace to my advantage.

I went up a flight of stairs right behind Vince, taking them two at a time. Other wedding guests were still behind me, catching up and overtaking. I pushed on.

We were heading for the back of the house, toward where Quentin's room had been and far away from Geoffrey's replacement honeymoon suite at the front of Raven's Bluff.

The wedding was in tatters. Yet again. My rivals were going to mop this up, but the thought at the forefront of my mind was how badly I had failed if yet another person had been killed.

At the top of the stairs, wheezing and out of breath, I took a second to lean on the banister. I needed more than a second.

Being a gentleman, Vince waited. He showed no sign of needing to breath heavily from his exertion.

Mindy reappeared, coming back along the first-floor hallway to collect me. Her face told me things I didn't want to know.

Forcing myself back to upright, I wheezed, 'Who is it?'

Mindy bit her lip. 'It's Geoffrey Banks.'

I felt an odd sensation where my eyesight went a little fuzzy and I couldn't hear what anyone was saying. The next thing I knew, I was looking up into Mindy's face and the right side of my head was wet and a little sticky.

'*Wake up, Felicity,*' barked Buster, right in my ear.

'What happened?' I mumbled, shoving my dog away as he tried to lick my teeth. The mystery of my wet face had been solved at least.

'You fainted,' winced Vince, leaning on the same piece of banister I had been until just a second ago. He looked uncomfortable.

'I did not,' I argued.

Mindy said, 'I'm afraid you did, Auntie. You almost took a tumble backward down the stairs too.'

My eyes widened in horror. I had a vague memory of teetering on the top step. Then a worrying question surfaced. 'Who saved me?'

'That would be me,' said Vince, still looking uncomfortable.

I groaned. The last thing I wanted was the well-dressed pirate to be able to claim I was in his debt.

'Why does he look like that?' I asked my niece, whispering so Vince wouldn't hear my question.

Mindy sniggered. 'He tried to give you mouth to mouth and you twitched your knee at an inopportune time.'

'Yeah,' groaned Vince, doing his best to stand up straight and not cup his bruised wotsits. 'You have bony knees, darling.'

I got an elbow under my body and let Mindy lever me off the carpet. 'You need to stop calling me that,' I warned Vince, meaning it wholeheartedly yet convinced he wouldn't listen.

'Yes, dear,' he pushed off the wall, and started along the hallway. He did so with a painful exhalation of air that made me feel good inside.

The memory of Mindy's news flooded back like an uppercut, making my eyes go whirly again.

Mindy grabbed my arm. 'Auntie, Geoffrey's not dead,' she tried to soothe me. 'Someone clonked him over the head. There's a brass candlestick on the floor. It looks like he staggered a few feet before he keeled over.'

Hurrying again, and taking deep breaths because I thought it might stop me from passing out, we hustled our pace until we found the gaggle of people gathered at the doorway to a room.

'It's the library,' hissed Mindy, as we squeezed through the press of people to get inside.

'In the library with a candlestick,' I murmured to myself. It was a daft cliché. All I needed now was a suspect called Miss Scarlett.

Geoffrey was sitting on the floor, propped against a bookshelf. Anton was next to him, holding his hand while Ian Riggs stood shirtless over them both. His shirt was in his hand, being used as a makeshift bandage to mop up the blood. Red stained Geoffrey's fine pink jacket and white cotton shirt. There were drips on his trousers too and a small pool on the carpet.

Seeing me approach, Geoffrey said, 'I don't know who it was, if that is what you are going to ask. I didn't see them. All I got was a sense that there was someone behind me. Then BAM! I came to with people around me.'

I knelt at his side. 'What were you doing by yourself? Everyone was supposed to stay in groups.' I was ready to thank the Lord that he was still alive and seemed relatively unharmed despite the alarming amount of blood on display. I was making a good point though.

Geoffrey closed his eyes. 'I was with Anton, Nat, Ian, and Ryan. We got separated when Anton said he thought he heard something. We were on our way back to the ballroom to get food. I popped my head in here and the next thing I knew …'

Anton offered me worried eyes. 'The cut on his head is really bad. I think he needs stitches.'

'I'll be fine,' mumbled Geoffrey. 'It's just a little blood. I'll wear a hat for the ceremony tomorrow.' He was making a joke, but the wedding itself was starting to look less and less likely.

Trying my best to keep a level head and to think like a detective, I scanned around the room until I spotted the candlestick Mindy mentioned.

'We need to bag that for evidence. Has anyone touched it?'

'I did,' admitted Anton, guiltily. 'Sorry, I didn't think. I just picked it up when I came in. I was terrified the killer might still be here. Why would someone target us like this? What have we done?'

His question prompted my mind to recall the homophobic filth Eric and Hattie felt it necessary to throw around. Anton and Geoffrey hadn't done anything, not by being honest about their sexuality, but what if the killer did have a reason for the attack?

If so, how were Quentin and the mystery man connected to it? Now was not the time for questions, not so far as I was concerned. I wanted to get Geoffrey back to his room where he could be made comfortable.

Standing up and backing away a pace, I asked the room, 'Does anyone know how to do stitches?'

Utter Confusion and Horror

To my surprise, Ian Riggs used to be a paramedic in the Army before fame found him. We didn't have any catgut to hand, but Ellis found a pot of superglue which Ian proceeded to use to seal up the head wound. A first aid kit – also supplied by Ellis – provided bandages and some duct tape finished the job, ensuring the improvised dressing would stay on Geoffrey's head.

'There is surprisingly little swelling,' Ian commented as he tried to close the wound. 'The blow must have been a glancing one. You were lucky.'

Geoffrey chuckled, then winced. 'Oooh. Mustn't laugh,' he winced again with his eyes closed. 'I don't feel very lucky.'

'No, you most likely don't' agreed the former paramedic. 'Still, I think this could be a lot worse. The skin split so neatly one could almost think it was made with a knife.'

The wedding guests began to drift away, but they did so in clusters or clumps, sticking together for safety because there was a killer in the house, and no one knew who it was. Nevertheless, there was dinner waiting for those who were yet to get their evening meal and that was enough to convince them to return to the ballroom and central area of the house.

Vince produced an evidence bag from a pocket of his perfectly tailored suit – he said he always kept a few with him, along with rubber gloves for picking up evidence. According to the private investigator, these were standard tools for someone in his line of work.

The brass candlestick went into a bag and was sealed for the police. Vince even took a bunch of photographs.

I wanted dearly to ask Vince to take over and be the one investigating. It was what he did for a living, but pride was stopping me. Stupid pride. I don't think of myself as a stubborn woman. Genuinely, I don't think I am, but I was being stubborn now.

Two deaths with no apparent reason or connection and now what looked like a considered attempt to murder Geoffrey. If only I could find out who the mystery man was, maybe that would give me a clue.

'Vince,' I called out his name to get his attention. 'Did you hear anything back from your friends in the police about the mystery man downstairs?'

He tutted and huffed, taking out his phone to check it before saying, 'Not yet. They will get to it. I'll give them a call and see if they can spare me a few minutes to run it through their system now.'

I let him get on with that and turned my attention back to my grooms.

'How are you feeling, Geoffrey?' I came down to one knee so I was at his eye level.

He shrugged, then winced at the pain doing so created. 'I have a corker of a headache,' he winced again. 'I think lying down somewhere dark might be in order.'

The decision to send them back to their room and have food brought up to them was made on the spot. People were standing by to help out when they were ready, the wedding guests, for the most part, only too willing to chip in where required.

'Shall we get you back to your room then? I suggested. 'Perhaps for safety we should move the party up to your suite.'

'Some party,' huffed Anton, helping Geoffrey to his feet. 'How many of us will be left in the morning?'

No one answered his question. How could we possibly? With help from Ian Riggs who was still without a shirt, Anton guided a rather wobbly Geoffrey from the room.

I followed on behind, Buster trotting happily by my side now that we were going at a walking pace and I thought for the first time in what felt like ages, about my cat, Amber. She was somewhere in the house, attempting to do the impossible and identify Quentin's killer.

How long had it been since I last saw her? It felt like hours, but checking my watch, it wasn't even sixty minutes since she ducked back into the gap behind the fireplace.

We walked by windows looking out over the island, the view obscured by the darkness, but there was no hiding the fact that the storm still raged outside. The rumbling thunder, howling wind, and indescribable flashes of lightning all served as a reminder for just how trapped we all were. There was no safe way off this island and also a sense that it wasn't safe to stay here either.

Startling me, the sound of a phone ringing cut through the relative quiet without warning.

It was Vince's.

He put it to his ear without slowing his pace. 'Vince Slater.' The conversation was one sided, the only word Vince spoke after saying his name was, 'Thanks.' When the phone went back into his inside jacket pocket, he announced, 'That was the police. They were unable to identify our dead mystery guest.'

'What does that mean?' asked Anton, confused.

Vince replied, 'Only that the man has no criminal record. When they get here, the coroner will be able to work out who it is from his dental records most likely. Plus, someone will report him as missing. It should not take the police too long to identify who it is.'

That hardly helped us in our current situation though. 'We need to work out who it could have been.' I voiced my thoughts.

Vince turned his head my way. 'You mean who could have attacked Geoffrey?'

Mindy grasped the idea. 'We could do a process of elimination. There were people in the bar or ballroom and there were people in other parts of the house. We ought to be able to narrow it down quickly to just a few people,' she ventured brightly.

Buster said, *'I'm getting that smell again.'*

'What smell?' I asked him aloud and without thinking.

Everyone turned to look at me with raised eyebrows and questioning looks.

Buster didn't notice and carried on talking. *'The woman smell from the first victim.'*

We were just arriving at the door to the grooms' suite, and as I looked down at Buster, wondering why he might now suddenly be able to smell Emma, Anton opened his door and screamed.

The pitch of it cut through me, filling me with terror. It also made me whip my head around to see what had caused the noise which is how I got to see my second hanged body in the same day.

Emma was dangling from the exposed wooden joists just like Quentin had been. This time there was no question she might have committed suicide. Her hands were tied behind her back.

Mercifully, she was facing away from the door but there was no questioning who it was that we could all see.

'Cut her down!' cried Geoffrey, sounding distraught.

Anton darted forward to get under the poor woman as she dangled, and Vince ran across the room to where the length of rope was tied to one of the bed feet.

Ian Riggs helped Geoffrey to slump to the carpet where he propped himself against the doorframe. He was wailing with grief and inconsolable.

'Oh, my sweet Emma. Who could have done this to her?' Geoffrey's words were only barely intelligible, contorted as they were around his anguished tears.

My hand was to my mouth, the horror of the sight before my eyes enough to stifle anything I might have wanted to say. A fourth victim and a third murder all in the space of a few hours.

Mindy was equally stunned. 'Auntie, who's doing this?' she asked fearfully. The investigation had been fun for her when we started, but the excitement she felt initially was long forgotten now.

Between them, Ian, Anton, and Ryan lowered Emma to the carpet. I didn't for one second believe there was any life left in the woman, yet I held my breath as the former paramedic checked her for signs of life.

There were none.

Three dead.

I could barely think straight.

Buster moved toward her, stopping only when I grabbed his hips.

'*I just wanted to get a sniff,*' he told me with a low whining noise. '*Maybe there is a scent of her killer still on her clothing.*'

Good point. I kept my hands on him, not wanting the others to think he was doing anything weird but moved across the carpet with him until he said he was close enough.

Buster sniffed the air, straining his nose forward to get it as close to Emma as possible. Geoffrey was weeping quietly by the door still, his head down and his eyes closed, and everyone else was just stunned into silence.

The only sound in the room was Buster's little piggy snorts as he sniffed and sampled the air.

'*I can smell her scent,*' Buster gave running commentary. '*It stands out because it is floral. The other scents here are musky. I can smell Vince and the other men, but I'm not getting anything else. There isn't another scent on her that I can detect.*'

I tugged at his hips a little, just enough to encourage him to move back; no one would appreciate my dog getting too close to the body.

After a few seconds, and with a grunt of anger, Vince pushed himself off the carpet. I had to question if he was blaming himself for this latest death. He could have insisted he investigate, but chose to defer to me when I argued.

Now a woman was dead, and her ex-husband had been attacked. Did we consider that to be attempted murder? Was he supposed to be dead too?

'Where did the rope come from?' asked Ian, standing up and stepping back.

I gulped and ran from the room, dashing along the hallway to the next door ten yards away. It was locked, of course and I had to wait for Ellis to open it for me.

Quentin's form lay there still, under the sheet and unmoving, but the rope he'd been hung with was no longer visible. It had been pushed to one side by the window, discarded but there for the police to inspect and remove as evidence.

The killer had recovered it and used it to kill Emma in the same manner as Quentin. Shaking my head in bewilderment and shaking all over from the shock of our latest awful finding, I staggered back to the grooms' substitute honeymoon suite.

There, I arrived in time to see Vince yank the top sheet from the bed and use it to cover Emma's form.

Two bodies found in the honeymoon suites - that could not be coincidence. Someone had targeted the grooms. That was especially obvious when you factored in the attack on Geoffrey. My mind whirled and spun, unable to make sense of the information it was being presented.

Anton, less affected by Emma's murder than his intended, Geoffrey, huffed a deep breath out through his nose as if to settle himself. Then he posed a question.

'When was the last time anyone saw Harold?'

Dominant Male

Vince stepped in to take control, no longer content to sit in the backseat just to indulge me.

'Everyone, I feel it is time I made my profession known. I am a licensed private investigator.' He took out his business card to show it around. 'Until the police get here, we need to preserve as much evidence as possible. We have multiple homicides and at this time no clue who the killer might be. I propose we not only lock these doors but place a guard in this hallway.'

Buster barked, *'Pick me! Pick me! Devil Dog will lurk in the shadows waiting for danger to present itself.'*

Ian Riggs spluttered. 'You can forget asking me to stand guard. I'm going back to my room with Ryan where I plan to barricade the door until the police get here.'

Ryan agreed wholeheartedly with Ian's plan.

Vince offered no argument. 'If it falls to me to stand guard then so be it. We need to seal off the library where Geoffrey was attacked so the police can inspect that too, and the blood you say you found on the banister.' He turned to me. 'Then I think we should go with Mindy's plan to establish where everyone was.'

'What if the killer isn't one of the guests and is a person moving around the house who none of us know about?' My question caused a muttering of nervousness from Ian, Ryan, and the two grooms.

Vince tipped his head to acknowledge my point. 'Then our efforts will fail to reveal who that person is. We should still do what we can to identify who was where, don't you think?'

Buster crossed the room to stand next to Vince, looking up at him and lifting a paw to pat at his shin, he said, '*I vote for any plan that brings Devil Dog into close proximity with danger. If necessary, I will engage in a fight to the death so the rest of you can escape. Devil Dog knows no fear.*'

'Good grief,' I sighed. Then, because people were looking at me again, I added, 'I think we should do exactly as Vince suggests.' To Ian and Ryan, I said, 'It would be helpful if you could come down to the bar for a few minutes now, just so we can record where you were and when. I suspect others will want to retire to their rooms too when we break the news about Emma.'

Geoffrey levered himself off the floor. 'We need to find Harold too,' he commented with a wince.

Anton gasped, 'You don't think he could have done it. Do you?'

Geoffrey pursed his lips, looking angry when he said. 'I intend to find out. Either way, I haven't seen him for a while, and I think he deserves to know. How he reacts might tell us whether he did it or not. He's not an actor, after all.'

Something about Geoffrey's final sentence lodged in my head, but it was a different thought that made it to my lips.

'We might have to do a full head count and make sure no one else is missing. Anyone not with the group now is either possibly the killer, or a potential target.'

Anton hooked an arm under Geoffrey's. 'I need to get this one lying down somewhere. He's in no shape to take part.'

The grooms were taking a battering, physically on Geoffrey's part but emotionally for sure as well. My heart went out to them both. Who could have predicted any of this? What to do though? They had already been through two rooms.

'You should take him to my suite,' I offered. Mindy and I will return later to clear our things out.' I shot my eyes at my niece to make sure she wasn't going to argue. It didn't look as though the thought had crossed her mind.

Anton and Geoffrey both thanked me, commenting once again about my willingness to go above and beyond that which might normally be expected of me. They departed with Ellis, Ian, and Ryan, with Mindy leading.

A few minutes later, I was back downstairs with Vince and Buster, where the smell of food made my stomach rumble. It was empty and needed filling. The two chefs sent to prepare for the feast tomorrow and ensure the early arrivals were fed this evening, had laid on a sumptuous feast including lobster and steaks freshly cooked to order on a hotplate set up in the ballroom.

Honestly, I didn't feel like eating, but I knew I would regret it if I didn't at least put something in my belly.

Most of the wedding guests were in sight, some eating, some sitting around chatting having already finished their meals and there were more in the bar area. A quick head count told me it accounted for almost everyone. I didn't spot Harold though which begged a question as to his whereabouts.

I'd been witness to his unpleasant side – so had everyone else when he all but attempted to drag his girlfriend from the room. It didn't make him her killer, but I couldn't deny my desire to find out where he might have been since she was last seen alive.

Vince strode confidently to the centre of the ballroom and called loudly to get everyone's attention.

'Ladies and gentlemen, most of you do not know me. My name is Vince Slater. I am a licensed private investigator and I find myself in need of your cooperation. There is no easy way to tell you this,' he paused to look around the room. He had complete command of all the people in it, their faces turned to watch him and hear what he was going to say next. 'There has been another murder,' he announced with suitable gravity to his voice.

The five words garnered the response one might expect: gasps, cries of surprise, a dropped fork that clattered noisily to the floorboards.

Before anyone could ask a question, Vince ploughed on, 'The victim is Emma Banks, the former wife to Geoffrey Banks, one of the grooms this weekend. As I am sure you are all aware, Geoffrey was also attacked. I am not drawing any conclusions at this time though it seems likely the attack on Mr Banks was an attempt on his life.'

There were further gasps.

Vince turned slowly on the spot, meeting eyes as he looked around the ballroom. A dozen people had food in front of them, but no one was eating; they were all too captivated.

'I must ask for your cooperation as we attempt now to establish where everyone was at the time of the attack on Mr Banks. I am also asking for anyone who saw Mrs Banks in the last hour to come forward. I wish to frame a timeline of events in this house as best as I can and work out how long ago she was last seen alive. Someone in this house has killed three people and attempted the murder of a fourth.' All around the room, eyes were shooting here and there, looking at the other people as each person present asked themselves who the killer could be. 'Staying in the bar or ballroom might be the safest course of action for you all. However, before someone points it out, I have no authority to demand you do so. If you wish to leave, no one will attempt to stop you, but I advise anyone choosing to not be here to barricade themselves in their room. The police will be here as soon as the storm permits.'

'When will that be?' demanded Nat Spanks, clearly expecting an answer.

Vince gave her a hard stare, forcing her to clam up. 'As I was saying, the storm is preventing anyone from getting to us. My concern is for anyone who is not currently in this room. We need to do a head count and work out if anyone is missing.'

'Harold is,' pointed out Edward Tolley.

'That's at least one person unaccounted for,' Vince told the assembled throng. 'Anyone not here could be lying injured somewhere much as Geoffrey was. We need to form search parties and check the house for anyone for whom we cannot account.'

His suggestion was greeted by groans from many. Some of the wedding guests, offered a free bar, had made good use of it and were well on their way to being of little use. Others just didn't want to play along any longer.

'You can get stuffed,' remarked Nat Spanks, voicing her opinion loudly. 'Geoffrey was with people when he got attacked. I'm not going anywhere. Not with some crazy killer stalking the house.'

'He wandered off,' I assured her. 'That was when he got attacked. Had he stayed with the others, he might have been protected. We need to find Harold and anyone else who is missing.'

'Ha! You can count me out,' Nat Spanks sat down again and picked up her drink; she had no intention of taking any further part.

'I'll be looking for volunteers shortly,' Vince announced. I didn't think he was going to get very many.

Having said that which he wanted to, Vince crossed the room to where Quentin's laptop and camera had been placed. Pausing for a second, he fished in a pocket for a fresh pair of white latex gloves, then flipped the lid open.

A creeping sensation made me look around the room, my eyes searching. I choked out an exasperated sigh that got the attention of those around me, Mindy in particular as she returned to the ballroom with Ellis Carter and came to stand by my side.

'What is it, Auntie?'

I blew out a sigh that made my lips flap as I let my shoulder slump.

'Where's Kevin?'

In the excitement of hearing there had been another attack – the one on Geoffrey – we all ran to see what was happening and he came with us. I hadn't seen him since. When I arrived in the library, there were more than a dozen wedding guests there and too much going on for me to notice Kevin had chosen to abscond. He might be guilty of nothing more than stealing Quentin's laptop and camera, but he was nowhere in sight now.

Mindy swore, choosing colourful words to punctuate her own feelings on the matter. I might not repeat her choice of phrase, but I held the same sentiment.

Vince heard her and met my eyes, mouthing something to himself that wasn't much removed from what Mindy said.

We were not doing very well.

Cats

Momentarily frozen by indecision, I stared into space as I tried to work out what I ought to do now. Under normal circumstances, by which I mean if the wedding hadn't turned into a bloodbath of murder and suspicion, I would be checking over the flowers, liaising with my master of ceremonies, Justin, and performing the thousand and one checks running a seamless wedding demanded.

Not only was there very little of that which I could do, there was also little point. Would the ceremony even go ahead? Or would this be my second total bust in a row? Selfishly, I allowed myself a moment of indulgent personal woe. I worked so hard to be the best at what I do, it was unfair that I should now find myself embroiled in diabolical murder and mayhem.

Mindy tapped my arm, breaking my reverie.

'Auntie, we should get something to eat,' she suggested, trying to get me to come with her to the hotplate. 'The chefs will want to pack up soon.'

I nodded my assent and followed her. Charles Blakely, another actor, and his wife, another writer, were being handed steaks when we arrived. They moved away with their food, making space for us.

The chefs were a man and a woman, both aged around thirty and both from a team of venue chefs called Premier Catering Services. I had used them many times in the past and recognised the faces of the two people serving food. I could not recall their names though.

'Hello,' I smiled at them both. 'Did you get everything you expected in the delivery this afternoon?' Checking the delivery was just one more item on my list of things I hadn't gotten around to doing yet. I always made sure the chefs had been correctly catered since I handled all of that too.

'Yes,' replied the man, meeting my smile. His female colleague was carving steaks from a large piece of sirloin. Mindy was there now, indicating with her hand for the woman to move the knife a little to the left before she started cutting – Mindy wanted a thick steak.

Hearing her male colleague's reply, she looked up. 'Well, almost, Freddie,' she argued.

I hitched an eyebrow at the man, encouraging him to explain. 'We are missing eggs, flour and a few other things. We didn't want to trouble you with it,' Freddie shot a glance at his fellow chef. 'Did we, Sally?'

Sally's cheeks flushed, so too Freddie's. They had discussed what to do and agreed a course of action that omitted involving me, the person paying their firm to get things done. It wasn't the right thing to do; I was always happy to be given bad news provided it was timely and gave me the chance to fix the issue. I got upset when people hid things from me until it was too late.

'I'll need a complete list,' I replied, my tone suggesting I wasn't interested in discussing the matter. 'Did Kevin explain why his load was short?'

Freddie cocked his head to one side. 'Well, that's just it. He said he had everything, but when he went back for the final pallet, we never saw him again. I went outside to look, but he was nowhere in sight and the van was locked up. The storm was coming in hard by then, so I didn't hang around to search for him. I figured he must have needed the loo or something and would reappear shortly.'

'But he never did,' I concluded.

Freddie puffed out his cheeks a little. 'No. He never did. I spotted another chap wearing the same logo just a short while ago - a big muscular lad, but he vanished before I could ask him about it. Anyway,' Freddie gave me a bright smile, 'it is all minor items that are easily replaced in the morning. One of us will take a run to the mainland for supplies as soon as the causeway is open.'

I was listening to him talking about getting the supplies, but his words were not sinking in. My brain was stuck on what he said about Kevin and then the other chap in the same uniform.

Unable to take my eyes from Freddie's face, I spoke to my niece.

'Mindy, have you got that photograph there?'

Mindy was staring at the hotplate as her inch-thick steak sizzled. 'What photograph?' she asked absentmindedly, her eyes never drifting from the juicy piece of meat.

With my heart beating in my chest and my nostrils flaring, I tried to stay calm when I replied.

'The one you took of the mystery man.' I was staring at Freddie still and beginning to freak the poor man out. 'What does Kevin look like?' I asked him.

Freddie was surprised by my question but flicked his eyes up and right as his memory engaged. 'Kind of skinny. He has long brown hair and a big mole by his left ear.'

I had stopped listening when he said the word 'skinny' because I now knew how greatly I had failed.

Mindy was breathing fast too. She'd heard the description and knew what it meant. When the picture app opened on her phone, she held it up for Freddie to see.

Sally squeezed in next to him so she could see too.

'Yeah, that's the fella,' laughed Freddie. Then what he was seeing reached his brain. 'Wait, he looks …'

'Kevin killed Kevin!' blurted Mindy, making the correct connection but in a highly confusing way.

I felt dazed when I added up all the clues that had been right in front of my eyes. 'It's why his clothes didn't fit properly,' I murmured, remembering how tight the delivery driver's arms had been inside his company jacket. His trousers too. 'He killed the real delivery driver and took his clothes.' I could see it now. He must have got wet, maybe after he killed Quentin and was trying to escape the island. The storm stopped him, and he came back, but by then we had found the body.

He killed the real Kevin and stole his clothes. Did he do that because his own clothes were wet or because he needed to disguise himself? It didn't matter either way because I felt certain Kevin's murder was opportunistic.

I started voicing my thoughts out loud. 'He came here to kill Quentin but couldn't then escape. He killed the real delivery driver and took his place, hiding the body and discarding his own wet clothes so he could pass unnoticed until the storm passed.'

Vince could hear me and was coming my way. He was adding things up too. 'That's why he took the laptop and camera,' he guessed. 'Or the reason to kill Quentin must have been something to do with what was on his laptop because it's been wiped. The hard drive is blank.'

'He wasn't a thief at all,' I mumbled to myself.

'He fooled me too, Felicity,' Vince admitted kindly. 'He's a good actor. But if this is about Quentin, why did he then attack Geoffrey and kill Emma?'

'Wait,' said Mindy, her face scrunched in concentration. 'Could he have attacked Geoffrey? He was with us when they found him.'

Vince pursed his lips as he considered Mindy's point, but I was ahead of him.

'I noticed he wasn't with the wedding guests when they set off to search the house.' I felt guilt admitting it as if what happened was somehow my fault. 'He appeared later but he had time then with no one's eyes on him to murder Emma and attack Geoffrey. Maybe he was the one who caused whatever it was that distracted Anton's group and split them up. He snuck off, killed Emma and then tried to kill Geoffrey.'

Any follow up question Mindy or Vince might have wanted to pose died a startled death when someone in the ballroom squealed in fright and then laughed.

I glanced their way, as did everyone else only to find Irina Kalashnikov pointing at a cat.

'I thought it was a giant rat!' she cackled. 'It made me jump.'

The cat, a large ginger and white tom with a scar on its nose, strolled into the middle of the room. Remembering Amber, I wanted to ask where it had come from, but before I could say anything Buster shot by me.

'Death to all cats!' he barked, haring across the dancefloor in the middle of the ballroom.

The cat meowed, and before the disbelieving eyes of every human in the room, the walls began to bleed cats.

Boris said earlier he didn't know how many there were living in the house, so let me tell you the answer is a lot.

Cats sprang from every direction. Fat ones, skinny ones, grey, tabby, white, black, blotchy, and even a couple of mangy old ones with chunks of fur missing. Twenty, fifty, maybe even a hundred cats shot out from the unlit fireplace, a small hole in the stage at one end of the ballroom, from between tables and chairs ... most of their entry points into the room were unseen.

Buster, moving about as fast as he ever can, applied the brakes in a panicked fashion. His butt hit the floorboards and his front paws attempted to dig in as he did his best to reverse course.

The cats were converging on the big ginger tom, which with other cats for reference, I could see was a considerable size.

Then I spotted Amber.

Just as Buster was skidding to a stop and trying to make his paws run back to me and the perceived safety I might offer, the ginger tom meowed again. I couldn't understand it, but everyone in the room heard several dozen cats all screech their compliance with his instruction.

Buster yelped and he kept yelping as he propelled himself away from the feline hoard. He was never going to make it though. Not designed for running at any speed faster than a sashay, the cats would outpace him before he got halfway to me.

Amber chose to save him. '*The stupid dog is with me,*' she told the ginger tom, sidling up to him in what I guessed was a sensuous way for a lady cat. She walked under the tom's nose, wafting her tail so it tickled under his chin. She was every bit his equal in size, her breed naturally a good percentage larger than the average household moggie. *'Please spare him.'* When the ginger tom failed to react, she added, *'I wish to kill him myself later.'*

The tom meowed again, and the cats ceased their pursuit.

It was a bewildering display, the animals behaving in a manner that defied what any human knew about them.

Buster continued to yelp all the way to Mindy's arms, my niece crouching to scoop him into the air where he panted, looked terrified, and licked her face for all he was worth.

Standing just a few feet away, Vince said, 'That has got to be the weirdest thing I have ever seen.'

I had to agree, but knowing it would attract the attention of everyone in the room, I nevertheless needed to speak with my cat.

'Amber,' I called to her. 'Amber come to mummy.'

Amber looked my way. *'What's with the baby voice? And since when were we related, Felicity. I'm a cat, in case you haven't noticed, a far higher lifeform in every respect.'*

Keeping the same tone, the one humans often use to talk to their pets, I tried again. 'Amber sweetie. Come away from all the other cats for a moment, won't you, dear?'

Eyeing me as if I were an imbecile, Amber ambled across the ballroom to get to me. The room was deathly silent though a few of the wedding guests had taken out their phones to film the odd event.

'*I came to tell you about the human who killed Quentin,*' Amber told me as she trotted across the floor.

I couldn't answer. At least, I couldn't easily think of a way to engage in a conversation with the cat without everyone present assuming I had lost my marbles.

'*He isn't here though,*' she said, frowning as she looked around. '*I convinced the king – that's what they call the top cat in any pack – to let the cat who saw the murder identify the killer. She says he isn't here.*'

I was racking my brain for a way to quiz her but everyone in the room was still watching me. With a jolt, it came to me, and I picked Amber up, hugging her to my chest and neck while snuggling my face into her fur coat.

Then, when her ear was really close to my mouth, I whispered, 'I think I already know who it is. I can't talk to you with all these people here. I'm going to take you somewhere private.'

Amber twisted her head around to look at the cats assembled in the middle of the dancefloor. Like a vicious gang of armed thugs, they looked surly and ready to dish out violence at the slightest provocation.

'*I will be fine from here,*' she told the ginger tom. '*I will find you again later.*'

Dropping her down from my neck so I had her cradled in my arms, I turned to Mindy and Vince. 'I'm going to put her back in our room. Mindy, do you want to come with me?'

Still holding Buster, though starting to strain a little under his weight, my niece grunted, 'Sure.'

Vince was looking at me with a strange expression. It was part curious, part accusatory, and filled with questions. He didn't say anything when I turned to go, but before I could take a step, he was shouting at someone else.

'Hey, what are you doing?' he growled.

Mindy and I both twisted our heads to find him stalking toward a young man now sat at the table with the laptop.

The young man was Hopster, the rap artist. He didn't look up, but he did reply.

'I'm retrieving the memory. At least, I'm trying to.'

Vince changed his attitude. 'You can do that? I mean, that can be done?'

Hopster didn't answer straight away. His partner Graham was leaning on the table, both men staring intently at the screen. When Vince arrived next to them, Hopster twitched his face up for a second.

'In theory. It depends if the person just deleted everything or if they used a magnet to wipe the drive. If they did the latter, there will be nothing left. Otherwise, we should be able to retrieve it all.'

I hadn't taken another step. I wanted to have the discussion with Amber, but I also wanted to see what was on the laptop.

Vince waved an arm at me, gesturing that I should just go.

'I've got this,' he assured me. 'I'll start piecing together who was where and who they were with and who saw Emma last. Ellis can help.' He volunteered the house manager, who accepted the burden without comment. 'You go ask your cat what she was able to find out.'

Startled by his instruction, I opened my mouth to say something but then couldn't work out what I could possibly say. I was going to do precisely that: go to my room where we would not be heard and get Amber to explain what she knew. Vince was looking at me in a way that made me wonder if he actually knew I could understand my cat and dog or was just guessing.

Closing my mouth once more, I swivelled around on my heels and left the ballroom, Amber still held to my chest.

Destruction

On the way up the stairs, Mindy sighed heavily, and I looked at her in question.

'It's always the pretty ones,' she sighed again. 'I was going to give Kevin ... I suppose I should call him fake Kevin now, my number. I guess I won't be doing that if he's a crazy psycho killer.'

She looked glum but to my mind she had dodged the proverbial bullet, finding out what sort of person he was before she could get to know him.

I checked around, glancing over my shoulders and listening to hear for anyone who might be around. I didn't think there would be anyone in the hallways, most of the wedding guests were in the ballroom, but that didn't mean the killer was and Harold wasn't in the bar either which meant he was somewhere else.

Could Harold be Emma's killer? I wouldn't put it past him, though what were the chances we had more than one vicious murderer in the house? It was a worrying proposition to consider. It made me think about Patricia Fisher and question how she ever figured these things out.

Convinced we were alone, I turned my attention to the cat in my arms. If she knew anything, I needed to extract that knowledge now. 'Amber, I think it was the muscular man in the delivery driver uniform. Is that who your feline friend saw?'

Amber twisted her head around to look at me. *'How should I know?'* she sighed in an annoyed manner. *'Cats don't pay attention to detail like what colour humans choose to use as their removable pelt. I brought the cat with me so she could identify him by sight and smell. Honestly, Felicity, you are dumb sometimes.'*

Mindy asked, 'What did she just say? It sounds like meows to me.'

Thinking my cat to be rather rude, I chose to not translate her words directly.

'Amber says she cannot identify a person from their description. She needs to put fake Kevin and the cat in the same room. Then the cat will be able to identify him.'

Mindy scrunched up her face a little. 'You keep saying cat. Does the other cat not have a name?'

Amber laughed. A human would have tipped back their head and guffawed, but Amber's laughter came to my brain without it passing through my ears. All her face did was gawp in shock at the question, her eyes on Mindy's face to see if my niece were being serious.

'*Cats do not have names,*' she replied, amusement in her voice. '*Cats have no need for them. I just explained this – we use sight and smell. Naming us is a daft human convention that domestic cats must suffer. The feral cats in this house would never stoop so low.*'

'Do dogs have names?' I found myself asking.

Amber curled her lip in disgust. '*Yes. Dogs love to have a name and feel loved by their human. It's soooo pathetic.*'

Buster, who had remained quiet thus far, happily trotting along next to Mindy, chose to snarl his opinion.

'*Dogs take names because we know we are part of a pack, a family, a community. We work with the humans, performing essential tasks we are better suited for than our two-legged counterparts. Cats are nothing much more than parasites. I have no idea why humans put up with your kind.*'

Amber chortled, flicking her tail lazily as she looked down at Buster's head. '*Humans worship cats because we are beautiful, Buster. Where dogs make mess and noise and create havoc, cats are refined. Where a dog requires constant effort, walks to the park, training, and entertaining, cats are independent. Cats are simply better than dogs and you should just accept it.*' Buster was getting mad, and I thought it a good thing she was finished. Unfortunately, Amber felt the need to deliver one final line. '*You fat, stupid, bone-breathed, fleabag.*'

Buster snapped. '*Let me at her!*' he barked, spinning around to block my path as he jumped to try to get to the cat in my arms.

Amber, uncertain she was safe, went vertical, climbing me like a tree. Her claws gave her traction as she escaped my arms to run up my jacket, onto my shoulder and then my head. Once there, she still didn't feel safe, so leapt into the air.

Buster followed, running along the hallway after the cat as fast as his stumpy legs could carry him. Amber easily outpaced him, of course. Buster's chances of ever catching her were slim to none, but that didn't prevent him hurling abuse and evil promises at her back end as she fled.

'Buster! No!' I yelled like a mad woman. It was a pointless gesture because he ignored me completely.

Amber rounded a corner, her tail the last thing to vanish. A few seconds later, Buster thundered after her.

Mindy's eyes were wide, but she had a grin on her face.

'That was fun. I take it they disagreed about something.'

I hurried after my pets. 'They disagree about everything. Honestly, it's a surprise every day when I get home and find the house still in one piece.'

To accentuate my point, a sound of something crashing to the floor sounded just around the corner. There came another crash a second later, a ferocious hiss from Amber and barking from my Bulldog. I shall refer to it as hissing and barking for though I could translate it, the language my animals were using would scare sailors from a bar.

Now running at full speed, I rounded the corner just behind Mindy who was skidding to a halt as she surveyed the destruction ahead.

A grandfather clock was lying on its side, the door to expose the mechanism no longer attached and some gears/cogs, which I suspected ought to be inside, had found new homes on the hallway carpet. An oil painting with a heavy frame was now on the floor, and it had a Buster sized hole through the middle of it.

That wasn't all though because further along I could see an occasional table which now had three legs and a tall ornate vase which was rolling lazily across the carpet on its side.

There was no sign of my pets.

Mindy wasted no time in trying to right the clock, but the task proved more difficult than she expected.

'How the heck did he knock this over?' she grunted, shifting position to get a better grip. 'It has to weigh more than a hundred pounds.'

I went to help her, but my gym-toned teenage niece had the clock in a squat position already and from there was able to easily lever it upward and back onto its feet. I collected the cogs, slipping them into the hole left by the broken door.

I picked the door up too. It had been snapped off at its hinges.

Buster reappeared, trotting back along the hallway, and looking proud of himself as he skirted around the fallen vase.

'*Heh, heh, that showed her.*' He paused before he got clear of the vase, and still panting from the effort of chasing Amber, lifted his back leg.

'Oh, no you don't!' I yelled, advancing on him, and having to step over wreckage to get there.

Guiltily, he lowered his leg. '*I need to go outside,*' he announced.

I waved my arms at the destruction left in his wake. 'We need to clean this up first, Buster. How did you manage to do so much damage?'

'*I'm Devil Dog,*' he boasted proudly, dropping his voice an octave, and growling so he sounded hoarse. '*It's what I do.*'

I held up the oil painting. 'Words fail me, Buster. I will have to replace this. How did you even get it off the wall?'

'*Devil Dog can achieve supersonic speeds. The vacuum left in my wake can have devasting consequences for stationary objects.*'

'What is he saying?' asked Mindy, standing the vase up and manoeuvring it back into position.

'Stupid things.' I gave Mindy a hand, but I didn't put the oil painting back up. I knew I would need to show Boris later, though quite how I would explain it and the clock and the damaged table I had no idea.

Content that I could do nothing more for now, I aimed a question at my dog, 'Where did Amber go?'

Buster gave me the canine equivalent of a shrug. '*I lost her somewhere further down the hallway. She's a slippery one. All cats are. There will be a reckoning later.*'

'No, there will not,' I argued, wagging my finger at him. 'You will be friendly towards Amber and I shall be having a word with her too when I find her.'

Mindy brought my attention back to more pressing matters. 'What's next, Auntie?'

It was a good question. We left the ballroom only so I could confirm with Amber about fake Kevin, but I hadn't even been able to do that. In fact, all we had really achieved, was causing damage to our host's house.

The obvious thing to do now was to return to the ballroom and once there see what assistance we could offer Vince. Alternatively, I could attend to the needs of the wedding party and their guests. That was what I came here for after all.

However, I chose a third option.

Accomplice

Since the grooms were now in my suite and I didn't want to disturb them unnecessarily, we found an empty drawing room with a desk at which I settled to consider what we knew so far. There was so much going on my brain was reeling from information overload. With luck, Vince was going to discover something on the laptop that would tell us why Fake Kevin targeted Quentin – assuming he did – and why he subsequently killed the real Kevin. It would still leave the attack on Geoffrey in question plus Emma's murder.

Before we returned to the ballroom and Vince, I wanted to review what I knew, or believed I knew, and get it straight in my head.

Mindy paced around the room counting off facts and guesses on her fingers.

'We know Fake Kevin is wearing real Kevin's clothes, so he is a prime candidate for real Kevin's murder.'

I agreed. 'Real Kevin was strangled. I think we are safe to assume the wet clothes we found thrown outside are Fake Kevin's. Fake Kevin looks strong enough to squeeze the life from a man.'

'But we are guessing he did that just to disguise who he is and probably use the delivery van to escape from the island?' Mindy concluded.

I nodded along. 'That makes sense to me. Poor Real Kevin just turned up in the wrong place at the wrong time.'

'So we think he came here to kill Quentin, but we don't know why.'

My phone rang. It was Vince.

'Yes?' I answered it cautiously, half expecting the rogue to whisper something naughty in my ear.

'Are you done? You might want to come back to the ballroom.'

'Why?' I wanted to know. 'What is it?'

Vince drew in a thoughtful breath through his nose. 'Proof that Fake Kevin knew Quentin.'

That bit of news was enough to get me moving. Three minutes later, Mindy and I were walking back through the ballroom.

The room still had most of the wedding guests in it. There was music playing and people were gathered in small clumps. They were quiet though, the party atmosphere that ought to be visible, completely chased away by recent events.

Matt Finn, looking like he might have had one too many, was stretched out on a Chesterfield sofa. His mouth hung open with a dribble of saliva running from one corner. Under an outstretched hand, a plate with dinner leftovers sat temptingly unguarded on the floor.

Buster spotted it and took a hard left turn.

'Oh, no you don't,' I grabbed the loose flesh at the back of his neck and sent Mindy to retrieve the plate.

Vince was across the room, watching to catch my eye. When I looked his way, he made it clear he wanted me to see what he had found.

Before I could get to him, Anton appeared in my path. He had his agent, Edward Tolley, with him.

'How are you feeling?' I asked the groom. 'How is Geoffrey?' I was surprised to find Anton here without his injured husband-to-be but made no comment.

I got a weak smile in return. 'Geoffrey has a corker of a headache,' he admitted. It came as no surprise. 'He fell asleep, so I locked him in the room and came to see what I could do. Neither of us have eaten, so I plan to get him a snack and head back up.'

Edward leaned in to speak quietly.

'Can the wedding still go ahead?' he asked, searching my eyes with his own.

It wasn't an easy one to answer. 'Well,' I started uncertainly. 'It's a civil ceremony, so all we need is the registrar to technically go ahead with the ceremony. I suspect that is not what you are asking though, is it?'

Anton frowned. 'Why would you ask about the wedding? Of course it's still going ahead.'

Edward looked embarrassed and unhappy. Answering my question, but talking to his client, Anton, he said, 'No, not really. I'm questioning what the public perception might be if we do go ahead. They might condemn us for it, and it's not like any of the guests will want to celebrate tomorrow. I think we might have to postpone.'

'What?' Anton's single word response had at least four exclamation marks after it. 'We can't postpone!' He raised his voice to make his point, silencing all other conversation in the room as everyone looked our way.

Edward tried to soothe him. 'Anton, what will the papers say? How can we have the pictures published to show your smiling face? The police will be all over you and Geoffrey tomorrow and Emma will be in the morgue.'

'No!' snapped Anton. 'This is our weekend. Our special day. We have to go ahead.'

Edward could see this discussion was drawing unwanted attention from the wedding guests in the room and that Anton was just going to argue harder if he didn't back down.

'Okay, Anton. Like Mrs Philips said, it is a civil ceremony, so technically there is no reason we cannot go ahead.'

'Then that is what we will do,' insisted Anton, his voice hard.

I moved out of the way, stepping back a pace to get clear of the argument. Anton's attitude was born of stress, of course. Weddings are habitually high-pressure environments even for those tying the knot. There are so many people to please, so many different elements to go wrong. He would calm down and see sense or he wouldn't. Either way, there was nothing I could do about it.

Anton had lowered his voice but was still arguing even though Edward had backed down.

'All we need to do is identify and find the killer. Once we deal with him, the police will want statements but will quickly finish with us and leave us to our nuptials.'

The way he talked about Fake Kevin made it sound like he planned to deal with him in person if he got the chance. I could understand the emotion, but the rage in Anton's voice made me feel uncomfortable.

I left him to snarl at his agent and walked across the room to where Vince was still waiting for me.

Vince kept his eyes on me all the way, which is a lot like being observed by a shark. It's not so much that I felt he was mentally undressing me, more that I suspected in his head he already had me naked and was getting on with what he believed would come next.

'Stop looking at me,' I demanded, growling at him from beneath an annoyed frown.

I got a snigger in reply. 'Don't be so deliciously attractive then.'

Mindy made a gagging noise behind me. 'I would say get a room, but you already have one.'

I spun around to face her. 'We do not! I have a room. He has …. arrgh! Why am I even engaging in this nonsense? Vince,' I put a finger to my eyes to stop the twitch again, 'what have you got to show me?'

He was still chuckling, mostly to himself, though Buster seemed to find him funny, when he lowered himself down on a chair next to Hopster. The young rap star was focused utterly on the screen of the laptop, his eyes flitting here and there to look at whatever it was that I could not yet see. Graham had pulled up a chair on the other side, and Ellis, seconded to Vince by Boris it would seem, stood behind them looking over the top.

Mindy and I went around the table to join the men and instantly saw why Vince asked me to come down.

Fake Kevin was on the screen.

'I recovered the files from the cloud,' revealed Hopster, too engaged in what he was doing to bother bragging – he was just telling us what he had done. 'There's more downloading still, the files are enormous – but we found this almost straight away.'

'How did you find it?' asked Mindy.

'Blind luck,' Vince grunted in reply. 'I asked them to work backward chronologically. These pictures are a week old.'

Kevin was a model, that much was obvious. In the delivery driver outfit, his muscle stretched the fabric, showing off just how much of it he had. In the pictures, he wore nothing but a tiny pair of shorts and some running shoes. If the intent was to show off his physique, then he achieved his aim. It's not something I ever found attractive, but I could acknowledge that his body was impressive.

Mindy had some dribble hanging off her bottom lip.

'Okay,' I broke the silence. 'So we have a connection between ... hold on, does it tell you his name.'

Hopster clicked the mousepad, making the pictures vanish. 'The file says Samuel Wilson and a date. I guess that's his name.'

'Samuel Wilson,' I repeated. 'That will do for now. So, we know Samuel knew Quentin, but why would a photoshoot result in the photographer's murder a week after the event?'

Vince scratched his chin. 'That is one of the questions we need to ask.'

'You have more?' I raised my eyebrows in expectation.

'How did he get here?' Vince asked. 'Ellis went through the cars and they were all accounted for.'

'They were,' Ellis sounded like he felt a need to defend his claim. 'We took a list of cars and then got everyone to say which was theirs. The only one we couldn't account for turned out to belong to Mr Slater.'

'So how did he get here?' asked Vince again.

All six of us were staring at each other, all daring someone else to say it first. After a few seconds, I could bear it no more, but when I spoke, so too did everyone else.

'He came here with someone!'

We didn't say it loud, but it was an inescapable conclusion. The reason he had no car was because he came here in someone else's. That meant there was at least one person here who knew precisely who Samuel Wilson was and had been covering for him.

Vince wasted no time, acting instantly.

'Everyone,' he called loudly. 'Your attention, please. There have been developments.'

'Oh, good Lord, who is dead now?' asked Nat Spanks, looking well lubricated. The free bar was not working in our favour.

Vince did not reply. 'The man who was found in a broom cupboard by Hattie was the delivery driver from the catering firm. His name was Kevin. I believe his killer to be the man you have seen here dressed in the delivery driver's clothes.' He paused and looked about the room before continuing. 'That man is called Samuel Wilson.'

Anton, his argument with Edward over, was at the bar getting a drink when he exclaimed jubilantly, 'You've identified the killer? That's marvellous!' Moving quickly, a pint of beer in his right hand, Anton rushed to see who it was.

Distracted by the groom leading a charge toward Hopster and Quentin's recovered laptop, Vince's speech got derailed.

Hopster looked up from the screen. It was one of the first times he had since I came into the ballroom, but just as he was turning the screen for

Anton and others to see, Anton tripped. I couldn't tell whether he slipped on a spill from someone's drink or if he found a raised lip on the ballroom floor, but he pitched forward, his arms flying out forwards in automatic defence and the almost full pint of amber liquid sailed into the air.

When I thought about it later, it seemed to happen in slow motion, but at the time, if I had blinked, I would have missed it.

The pint of beer doused the laptop like a bomber making a direct hit. Hopster caught a good portion of it too, the foamy wave hitting his shirt and splashing down his loose-fit jeans to drench his groin. The young musician leapt backward, knocking his chair over in his bid to escape the remaining liquid cascading off the table from all four sides.

'What the heck, man?' Hopster exclaimed, swiping at his crotch to send a shower of beer to the floor. 'Looks like I've wet myself,' he complained.

Anton was mortified. 'Oh, my. I caught my toe. I'm so sorry.'

Vince was holding the laptop up and at an angle. The screen had gone blank, and a small river of beer was running from the keyboard part of it. The look on Vince's face said it all.

It was dead.

Anton's hands gripped either side of his head. 'What have I done?' he wailed. 'Please tell me it still works.'

'*Mmmm, nice beer*,' said Buster, mopping up the spilled liquid with his tongue too fast for anyone to stop him.

Vince put the laptop back down. Something inside made a popping noise, and a small puff of smoke found its way out from beneath the keys.

'Does that answer your question?' asked Vince, his eyes never leaving the stricken computer. Anton looked set to burst into tears as Boris put an arm around his shoulders.

'What's done is done,' said Vince, turning around again to face the room, controlling the audience with his eyes. 'What we were able to learn from Quentin's laptop is that the man posing as the delivery driver had a link to both victims. He appears in pictures on the computer of the first victim and was wearing the second victim's clothes. However,' Vince narrowed his eyes as he scanned his audience, 'he was not alone. Someone brought him to the island today.'

It was a brash accusation levelled at no one in particular but also at everyone in the room.

People were talking in an instant, several of them quite vocally arguing with Vince – it wasn't them and how dare he?

He raised his hands to ask for calm, and when it didn't come, he bellowed, 'That's enough!' His voice shut off all the others like flicking a switch. 'We have three dead and one man with a head wound. There are several wedding guests missing still and the man we now know to be called Samuel Wilson, last seen wearing the uniform of a delivery driver from a catering firm, is at large somewhere on this island. Given the inclement weather, I expect he is in this house.'

Ian Riggs found his voice, 'What is it that you are proposing we do? Form a militia and search the house until we find him? Or are you going to subject each of us to questioning under a bright light until we cave and admit we are Samuel's accomplice?'

Having made a target of himself, Vince swung his attention toward the TV personality. Ian's boyfriend, Ryan Clarke, was at his shoulder in a show of support.

Vince asked him a yes/no question, 'Do you wish to see the killer caught?'

On the spot, with all eyes on him, Ian felt he had to answer, 'Well, yes, but …'

'Do you believe persons not currently in this room with us are safe? Harold Cambridge is somewhere in this house. If we assume he is still alive and not Emma Banks' killer, then I put to you that he is potentially unaware of his girlfriend's murder and also in grave danger.'

'Well …'

'Mr Riggs, will you choose to be a coward?' His last question hit the TV personality like a slap to the face. Vince didn't give the man time to react. 'I am sure that you will not. We have a moral obligation to find Mr Cambridge, to account for anyone else whose whereabouts and condition are not currently known, and we need to be sure we keep everyone safe until the storm passes and the police arrive.'

To my surprise, the next person to speak was Anton. He had shaken off Boris's arm and appeared to have regained his composure.

'Thank you, Mr Slater. I think we can assume this Samuel Wilson chap came here to murder. We may never know why, and that means we cannot be sure he has finished. I for one will not be able to sleep tonight unless I know we are all safe. You are my friends, my … wedding guests, and the ceremony will take place tomorrow in whatever form and at whatever time we are allowed.'

Vince dipped his head at the groom in thanks. 'Much like the search for evidence, I propose we all form groups and search the house. Before we do that, we need to perform a head count and be certain that no one has been overlooked.'

In the Clouds

Among those listed as not accounted for were the film stars Bruce Force and Lara Huntsman-Digby. They were probably still in their room doing … well, whatever it was, I did not wish to know the details. Harold hadn't been in his room for a while, but we would check there first when we set out from the ballroom.

Anton's little speech had done the trick to shame everyone into helping, but to my great horror and surprise, the wedding guests had chosen to arm themselves.

It was one of those ideas that begins as a whisper, 'I'd feel safer with something to defend myself,' and quickly gathers pace until more than two dozen slightly drunk people are holding kitchen knives, pairs of scissors … I saw Ian Riggs holding a large meat tenderiser.

It was a terrible idea, but as I thought about what I could say to stop the mob we inadvertently formed, I saw Boris appear with a pair of shotguns.

'Oh, my word,' I gasped.

Next to me, Mindy said, 'Yeah! This is more like it!' With a flick of her right hand, a pair of nunchucks appeared. 'Tooled up and ready to go. If I find Samuel, he's getting it right in the trousers.'

Buster nudged my leg. *I need a grenade launcher. One either side mounted along my flanks should do it.*

'Mindy put those away,' I insisted.

Her smile froze. 'Aww, Auntie.'

'Right now, please. Nunchucks are not a ladylike thing to own.'

167

She folded them into one hand and began to tuck them into the small of her back again. She was moaning grumpily under her breath, 'I bet no one would try to stop me if I had a penis.'

Buster nudged my leg again. He was sitting on his rump and using a paw to pat at me. *'I might need a helmet too, just to protect my face from the backwash. It needs to have a visor with a targeting system in it.'*

I walked away from him, heading for Vince. 'Vince I'm not so sure this is a such a good idea. Have you seen them all?'

Vince had, and was about as happy with it as I was. 'I don't see how we can stop them now. Not since one of the grooms is toting an elephant gun. We wanted them to search the house. Now they are going to do it.'

'But what if they accidentally shoot someone?'

Vince grimaced. He saw my point, but he wasn't planning to intervene. Boris and Anton were taking charge, dividing the wedding guests up and giving them different areas to search.

I went straight to them.

'Boris, I know this is your house, and Anton, this is your wedding, but the guests have all been drinking. What if someone gets accidentally hurt? They are all carrying lethal weapons, I pointed out. What if they bump into Samuel and decide to give chase?'

Boris looked around at the wedding guests. Egged on by Anton, who felt he had a personal stake in finding Samuel, people who would never think to brandish a knife were now play acting at tackling a murderous horde while they waited to leave the ballroom.

'I think Mrs Philips may have a point,' murmured Boris, quietly. He sounded worried. Quite rightly so in my opinion.

Anton, however, wasn't to be discouraged. 'Nonsense, old boy. It's nothing more than a precaution. No one is drunk per se. Just a little Dutch courage, that's all. It's my wedding tomorrow and no blaggard murderer, pretty boy model is going to ruin it.' He spun around to face the guests looking like a general ready to lead his troops into battle. 'Come on, everyone. Let's find our missing friends!'

Boris led one group, Anton another, and a third followed Ian and Ryan. When Ellis drew level with me, he paused to say, 'I'll do my best to keep them sensible.'

I watched them depart to search the house with serious doubt they were all coming back. It made me feel a little sick but running after Anton to demand he abandon this plan was only going to start a new round of fighting and we still needed to find the missing people, none of whom were answering their phones.

Accepting there was nothing I could do about it, I wanted to focus on something I could do. I turned away from the ballroom doors, intending to speak with Vince, only to find he was standing in my shadow. I bounced off his chest with my face and slapped his arm.

'What are you doing?' I demanded.

He shot me his killer smile. 'Drinking in the heavenly scent I always get whenever I am near you.'

'Oh, for goodness sake.'

Mindy, standing just a few feet away with Buster, rolled her eyes and gave me a look that said she didn't believe my claim to not be involved with Vince.

Vince stepped around me and spun to walk backward as he made his way to the doors. Over my head he called to Hopster and Graham.

'Chaps, are you ready?'

Hopster jumped to his feet. 'Sure. We need to start again. Let's get to it.'

'Quentin's laptop is dead, isn't it?' I asked in confusion.

Hopster mimed firing a shotgun at the computer to put it out of its misery.

'It sure is.'

'There's another way to carry on what we were doing,' explained Graham as Hopster lifted another laptop from a bag by his feet. This one had bullet hole stickers on it, and I figured it was probably his.

Tucking it under his arm, the young rap star came around the table. He was walking funny due to his rather wet pants.

'All the data is still in the cloud,' he told us. I nodded along as if I had the slightest clue what he was talking about. 'This Quentin guy must have a phone, right.'

'Of course,' said Mindy, instantly seeing what Hopster and Graham had planned.

I wanted to play along and pretend I understood but was too desperate to actually know what was going on.

'What?' I begged. 'What about the clouds?'

Hopster's eyes flared, looking at me with pursed lips as he questioned how to explain basic modern technology to the cave lady.

Mindy said, 'The phone will be linked. With it we can access Quentin's cloud of data and dump it to a new file on Hopster's computer. It will be like Anton's accident never happened.'

'We'll be starting the download again,' explained Hopster, 'So it will take us a little while to get back to where we were. Otherwise ...' He wriggled his hips. 'I could do with getting some fresh clothes actually. Does anyone know where Quentin's phone is?'

Low Point

Their rooms were not that far from each other at the rear of the house so while Hopster changed his clothes for ones not doused liberally with beer, Vince, Mindy, Buster, and I went to the honeymoon suite. The original one. That there were bodies in both rooms made me feel quite off kilter.

Mindy got to the door first. Well, actually, that is inaccurate, because Buster got there first, but it was Mindy who tried the door handle.

'It's locked,' she told us, pulling a face. 'Do I kick it in?' That my niece thought nothing of kicking in doors should tell you all you need to know about her.

'No need,' I let her know. 'We have a Vince.'

She cocked an eyebrow and took a step back. Vince produced a small leather wallet from an inside jacket pocket, and from it selected two thin tools. I'd seen him use them before, of course, when he chose to break into Orion Print a week ago.

Mindy had not and was fascinated.

When, three seconds later, the lock clicked and the door popped open, she was duly impressed.

'Coooool,' she gasped, peering at the leather wallet as Vince put it away. 'Where can I get …'

'Don't even think about it, Mindy,' I warned her. 'You are a wedding planner's assistant. Goodness only knows why you feel the need to bring nunchucks with you for a celebrity wedding.'

'Because people keep getting murdered, Auntie,' she choked out a tired laugh. 'If Samuel pops out and tries to kill us, you'll be glad I have them.'

I was simply too beaten by my day to mount an argument and Vince was heading for Quentin's body, so I let it go. 'Buster, stay here.' My dog was attempting to follow Vince; that he liked the suited pirate was obvious. He would have to get over him though for I had no intention of seeing the man again after we escaped this island. We are not compatible.

A noise behind me drew my attention, but just as my heartrate began to spike, I saw it was Graham and Hopster approaching.

'Any luck?' asked Hopster.

Vince stood up and turned around, a phone in his hand.

'It's dead,' he told us, jabbing at the screen with a big, meaty sausage finger. 'It probably just wants charging though.'

Graham clapped his hands together. 'Let's do it then. This place is freaking me out; I need something to distract me.'

They were all talking in the hallway, discussing what model of phone it was and working out who had a charger to hand that would fit it. I wasn't listening though. I was staring at the sheet covering Quentin's body.

Vince saw me and tracked my eyes.

'He was a friend of yours?' he asked me, his tone soft.

I sniffed and nodded. He was, but looking at the sheet that covered his body, I couldn't help but question how much I actually knew about him.

He had a wife and children, and he was a photographer, but something had resulted in his death. Was it his fault? Was it something he was involved in? Something he did? Samuel Wilson chose to track him to Raven Island and end his life. Was it to silence him?

'What is it?' asked Vince, picking up on the expression on my face.

I almost started talking about the thoughts that had just been in my head when a new one emerged. It screamed and jumped up and down, demanding I pay attention to it.

'How did the killer get him off the floor?' Vince tilted his head in question. 'He's not tied up,' I pointed out. 'Quentin might not be a big man but he's big enough to have fought back. Samuel had to get the noose around his neck and lift him from the floor and all the while Quentin just let him do it.'

Vince shook his head. 'He was most likely unconscious. The killer will have hit him over the head.'

'Is there any sign that he did?' I shot my question back at him fast enough that it caught Vince off guard.

He reversed direction, going back to the sheet where he lifted it slightly to peer at the form it hid. I wanted to see too, but not enough to make me actually do it. Vince put a knee down and then pulled the sheet back even further. He was examining the body, pulling on a set of gloves before he touched it.

'What's going on?' asked Hopster.

It was Vince who answered. 'Felicity might be onto something.' No one spoke for a moment, waiting for Vince to explain what the 'something' might be. He pulled the sheet back over Quentin and stood up, yanking off the rubber gloves with a snapping noise. 'There is no sign that he was rendered unconscious. That doesn't mean he wasn't,' Vince added hastily.

'I looked for a sign that he was injected with something. Even a tiny prick can leave a blood spot on a cotton shirt. Obviously, I haven't completed a full forensic examination, and it could be that Samuel used a sleeper hold to knock him out ...'

'But you don't sound convinced,' Graham summarised what the rest of us were thinking.

Vince shrugged, still staring down at the body. 'I don't know. There is something about this that just doesn't seem to add up.'

A growl from Buster made me jump. When I glanced down though, I found he was slowly backing out of the room.

I found out why the next second when a cat popped out from under the bed. It was joined a second later by another, and then two more. Then the big ginger tom appeared and a heartbeat later, Amber sauntered out.

'Amber,' I gushed, pleased to see my cat. 'Don't worry about trying to work out who the killer is. Just come back to Felicity.'

'*Does she have to?*' asked Buster, now hiding in the hallway and peering around the edge of the doorframe. '*She seems quite happy here. Why don't we just leave her?*'

Amber looked up at me. '*I thought you might be interested to learn the human who was in this room earlier, is now heading for the roof and there are people following him.*'

The news jolted me, not least because of the off-hand, disinterested way in which my cat delivered it.

'The one who killed Quentin?' I begged to know. 'Was the cat who saw him finally able to confirm who it was?'

'*Oh, yes,*' replied Amber turning her attention to a patch of fur on her shoulder. '*We've been following him for some time.*

'Where is he now!? Which way is it to the roof?' I was bouncing on my toes, ready to start running but without a direction to go in.

Amber turned away from me, her eyes locked on the ginger tom instead. Whatever passed between them didn't reach my head, but the cats started running the next second.

Amber zipped between our legs as we stood in the doorway, the other cats in front, behind, and to her sides as half a dozen of them burst into the hallway, turned left, and picked up speed.

Amber's voice echoed in my head, '*This way!*'

I started running, shouting her words as I started along the hallway at my best speed. 'This way!'

I got two paces before I noticed no one was following me. I turned around to find four faces staring at me with various expressions of disbelief and confusion. Only Mindy had a different look on her face; she looked embarrassed for me.

'Um ...' I stuttered. 'You all heard that, right?'

Vince cocked an eyebrow. 'You having a conversation with your cat? Yes. We all heard that.'

Amber's voice echoed down the hall as the cats left us behind. '*Are you coming?*'

I dismissed the looks I was getting and started running again. Over my shoulder, I shouted, 'I'll explain later.'

The cats were waiting at the end of the hallway, milling around as if uncertain which way they needed to go. As I came closer, I realised they were waiting for a human to open a door. They could move through the passages in the walls easily enough, but I could not then follow them if they did, and they were bright enough to know it.

'*Hurry up,*' Amber snapped at me impatiently. '*The king does not like to be kept waiting.*'

The door led to another hallway and a stairway going both up and down.

As I let the door go, a backward glance showed me the other humans had closed the lead I briefly created.

'Auntie, what's happening?' asked Mindy as she hit the door hard enough to slam it back into the wall.

Hopster came through next, his laptop still clutched under one arm. 'Where are we going?' he wanted to know. 'And why are we following a bunch of cats?'

'They found Samuel!' I shouted as I started up the stairs. I was getting out of breath again. 'The cats say he is heading for the roof and there are people chasing him.'

'The cats say?' Hopster's question was not unwarranted but I had neither the breath nor the time to explain things now.

The sound of a shotgun being fired meant I didn't have to. Everyone's eyes widened, shocked to hear such a noise. It boomed in the stairwell, muffled only slightly by distance and closed doors. It propelled all of us to run harder.

Even Buster was putting in a valiant performance, just about keeping up despite his disadvantages.

We charged up the stairs until we reached the next floor. We were near the top of the great house now, the view from the windows showed me a crashing angry sea and evil clouds hanging from a tormented sky.

Only a fool would go outside in it. The stairs ended at this floor, and the cats were ahead of us, looking up at the door that kept them from the hallway beyond.

There were raised voices coming from beyond – wedding guests, drunk or otherwise, were searching for Samuel and shouting instructions to one another.

Mindy got to the door first, thrusting it open to spew cats into the space beyond and now we could see wedding guests. They were coming our way and were led by Anton.

Spotting us, his face lit up for a second. 'Did you see him?'

'Samuel?' I tried to clarify though I felt certain that was who he meant.

'Yes,' Anton's voice was exasperated and angry. 'We flushed him out by accident. He's on the run and he's wounded. I think I winged him.' I couldn't help but notice how pleased he looked about it.

'*He went to the roof,*' said Amber. I glanced down to find there were new cats with us now. '*The king says there is a door the humans can use to get there.*'

I came very close to telling everyone what Amber had just told me, but Anton repeated his question.

'Did you see him? Did he come past you?' It was posed with malice behind the words and looking into his eyes, I could see a need for violence in them. He was in an agitated state and filled with rage. Whether it was because he believed Samuel had ruined his wedding or because he'd attacked Anton's husband-to-be didn't matter. Anton was leading an angry, drunken mob and if I told them where the young man was, I would have to share the responsibility for what then transpired.

'We haven't seen him,' I replied. It was an honest answer.

Anton growled his anger and frustration. 'Arrrgh. He must have doubled back. Ellis take half and go down to the next floor in case he tries to escape that way. We'll go room to room here and try to flush him out.'

Ellis, out of all of them, was the only voice of reason, 'Sir, this is folly! We should retire to the ballroom and leave this to the police. We are supposed to be looking for your missing guests.'

'Dash it all, man! If we catch the killer, we won't have to look for them. Neutralise Geoffrey's attacker and the danger will pass. I want people to be able to relax.'

Mindy leaned in to whisper, 'Auntie, I don't like how mad he looks.'

The crowd of people were splitting, roughly half running back along the hallway away from us, while the others followed Ellis. He looked reluctant, but if he didn't lead them, there were others in his group who were ready to take on the task.

Nat Spanks was brimming over with fiery justice. 'Come on, everyone! Let's get him.'

I held Mindy's arm, making sure she stayed with me as they pushed past us to go down the stairs we had just ascended.

From behind me, Hopster asked, 'What do you think they will do if they find him?' A tremor in his voice let us know he already knew the probable answer to that question.

Rather than reply, I said, 'I think he's on the roof.'

The cats were already moving, drawing me to the right and in the opposite direction to that which Anton had just gone.

Vince coughed, a deliberate act to get my attention. 'Felicity, dear, what is it you are proposing to do?' When I turned to look at him, he added, 'Assuming he is on the roof. What will you do? Apart from getting blown away by the storm that is.'

I didn't exactly have a plan, but I said, 'Samuel might have killed three people, but we know he has an accomplice. He needed someone to help him subdue Quentin.'

'Not necessarily,' Vince argued.

Not to be put off, I countered, 'But he couldn't get to the island by himself so whether he killed Quentin single-handedly or not, there still has to be someone lying about knowing who he is. If Anton, or someone else gets to him first, I don't know what might happen.' In truth, I had a fairly clear picture in my head for what I thought would happen, but it felt like saying the words might bring the vision to life. 'I'm going to see if I can find him. If I can, I want to keep him safe. The police should deal with him, not an angry mob.'

Buster stepped forward. '*Devil Dog at your service, Felicity. I will protect you should the miscreant attempt to do you any harm.*'

With a deep breath to steady myself, I looked at my niece. 'Mindy, can you look after Buster for me, please? I don't think it is safe for him to come up on the roof.'

Mindy looked aghast. 'No, Auntie! I'm coming with you.'

'Devil Dog laughs at the storm. Its might is no match for my power!'

'Vince?' I tried in vain for I knew for certain he was going to give the same answer.

He shook his head slowly from side to side and turned up the collar on his jacket. 'Let's do this together. Anton said he is wounded, that will make him scared and unpredictable. We will offer him sanctuary and pray that he sees sense.'

'I'll look after the dog,' volunteered Hopster, looking only too pleased to have a reason to not go up to the roof with us.

Graham got in on the action too. 'Yeah, I'll ... um, help.'

Vince paused to tell them, 'Find somewhere out of the way and let me know where you are.' He produced a business card from a pocket like it was a slight of hand magic trick. 'Recover the files, gents, and let's see what they show us.'

Buster was far from happy. *'Why are you ignoring me, Felicity? Devil Dog is ready for action!'*

'Because you're an idiot,' sighed Amber. 'And you look like a balloon animal ... after someone popped it.'

Buster swung his head to growl at his housemate, spotted the gang of cats all around her, and decided to hold his tongue.

'Please?' he begged me.

I came down to one knee to scratch his ears and stroke his chin. 'Not this time, sweetie. I don't want you to accidentally walk off the side of the roof.'

Mindy and Vince were already going through the door the cats were milling around in front of. None of the cats attempted to follow. Of course, it was raining outside; the cats were bright enough to stay inside in the dry and warm.

Brighter than me, apparently.

I ducked through the door to find Vince's back disappearing around the web of a spiral staircase. It wound tightly upward; stone triangles barely big enough for my feet leading to the roof.

A whoosh of cold damp air swept down, telling me Mindy had found a door at the top. I heard it slam open and pushed onwards, my hair already whipping around my head.

I heard a voice and thought it was Mindy's, but I couldn't hear what she said – the wind on the roof was enough to carry her voice away before it could travel back to me.

As I neared the top, the wind and noise grew in intensity. It was pitch black outside; the night sky devoid of stars as a thick layer of storm clouds hung over our heads. Chilly raindrops began smacking into me, stinging the exposed skin on my face and neck. I needed a winter parka to protect myself, yet as I stared into the darkness and saw what I thought was a man silhouetted on the roof fifty yards away, I knew I was going to have to just manage.

I shouted to Vince – he was closest, but he didn't react. I tried again, bellowing at a level that would soon render me hoarse and got the same result.

He was looking the wrong way. So too Mindy, both scouring the exposed flat areas of the roof and seeing nothing to pursue. Leaning into the wind, which kept switching direction as if it were deliberately trying to make me fall, I staggered across to Vince.

He was soaked already, but less so than I in my silly wedding outfit. He jumped when I got close enough to him to lunge and grab him as an anchor.

He pulled me into his arms so we could be close enough to hear each other without having to shout.

'I saw him!' I pointed across the roof.

The top of Raven's Bluff is an exposed space with a castellated edge going between small, pointy turrets at the corners. I say corners, but I could count five just to prove this was a folly. There was a large five-sided pyramid jutting into the sky from the middle of the roof and around that ran a ten-yard-wide flat surface. We had emerged in one corner, the spiral staircase rising up through the centre of the tower.

I jerked my arm at the spot where I thought I saw Samuel. It was all the way over on the far side. There was nothing there now, of course, but I knew what I had seen.

Vince cupped a hand to his mouth and around my ear as he said, 'Wait here. It's not safe to be moving around in this wind.'

'It's not safe for you then either,' I argued, grabbing his arm as he tried to move away.

He turned to me, smiling down with an expression that, for possibly the first time ever, didn't make me think he was trying to undress me. 'I weigh at least twice what you do, darling. I'll be back shortly.' Then, to ruin what was starting to feel like a moment, he ducked his head, stole a kiss, and smacked me on the bum for good measure.

What I shouted at his back got carried away by the wind, which was a shame because I wanted him to hear the names I called him.

He caught up to Mindy who had already reached the pyramid section of the roof and was making her way around it. I saw them exchange a few words, their heads close together, though in the darkness I could barely see them at all.

I thought for a moment they were going to split up, each going a different way around the pyramid. It would guarantee they caught Samuel if he were hiding on the other side, but also meant he would face only one of them. It would be brave, but foolhardy. Mercifully, Vince was more cautious with my niece than that, pointing to the right and going with her when she set off.

In seconds, I was alone. Soaked through, my feet squishing in my shoes and yet another outfit rendered unsalvageable, I started to back toward the stairwell. A flash of movement registered in the corner of my eye, making my pulse race even faster than it already was.

I spun around to squint into the dark. I saw nothing for a second, my brain telling me I was jumping at shadows, but before my heart could beat again, my eyes found a shape moving in the shadow cast by the pyramid. It was on the opposite side to the one Vince and Mindy had just vanished behind.

My feet continued to back toward the door in the tower and the suggestion of safety it provided, but my eyes were glued to the shadows, waiting for the shape to appear again.

When it did a moment later, I squeaked in fright. I wanted to run, but something about the way the shape moved held me back. It was struggling.

I took a pace toward it, hesitating as I continued to squint into the darkness.

Then Samuel emerged from the shadow. The night was dark, but not so devoid of light that I couldn't see he was injured. He'd been using the steep sloping side of the pyramid roof to keep himself upright. Now clear of it, his legs were carrying him across the roof and directly toward me, but he was in no shape to do me any harm.

Where were Mindy and Vince? I needed them now more than ever.

My heart hammered in my chest, making me feel faint and nauseous at the same time. I wanted to run – I believed Samuel had killed three people though I had no idea why. Would he attempt to kill me just to escape? Was he capable?

Anton boasted winging him with his shotgun – it looked a lot worse than that.

Unable to stop myself, I ran to him. Yet as I did so, I got a sense of motion behind me.

Catching Samuel as he all but folded into my arms, I twisted my head to see Anton and others flooding out of the tower. Most stayed close to the door, unwilling to venture too far into the storm, but Anton, the shotgun aimed loosely in my direction, stalked across the roof.

'He's hurt,' I yelled, feeling miserable and empty. Just minutes ago, we were chasing a killer, now I found myself cradling a desperately injured young man and all I wanted to do was protect him. I didn't know for sure that he had killed anyone, I only suspected.

Anton shouted, 'Get away from him!' and motioned with the business end of the shotgun that I should get clear.

Samuel had collapsed to the surface of the roof when I got to him and was lying across my lap now with his legs tucked awkwardly to one side as if forgotten.

I looked down at him as he looked up with terror etched in his face and I swear I saw the life leave his eyes. They rolled upward and the tension in his body melted away.

The rain continued to fall, matching my sense of helplessness and doing its best to wash away my tears.

If there is a low point in my life, I would knowingly claim it was hearing my husband had passed away in his sleep. But right now - that moment on the roof – it came a close second.

When I lifted my rain-soaked face to look at Anton, the rage he'd displayed earlier was gone. Relief had replaced it, blessed relief, but as Vince and Mindy found me, I couldn't help but question if that was an emotion anyone should be feeling right now.

Devil Dog Time

Vince teased me out from under the limp form, handing me off to Mindy before checking on Samuel and declaring him to be gone. He scooped the young man, carrying him carefully and with silent dignity back down the spiral staircase.

Anton wanted to check Samuel's condition for himself but a warning growl from Vince was all it took to make him back away. A few of the wedding guests, the more inebriated ones, looked pleased with themselves, but only briefly. When they saw my face, their smiles dropped away.

The blast from the shotgun had hit Samuel in his back as he ran away, and it looked as if the shot had penetrated his lungs. Whether he had bled out or drowned in his own blood was academic.

The next hour passed in a blur as events took place around me. I was disconnected from them, unable to shift the awful memory of … I looked down at my arms for the umpteenth time. Somehow, I could still feel Samuel's weight on them.

I was in the room we had hastily shifted my things to. My clothes were flung on the bed – there hadn't been time for anything else as we tried desperately to save the weekend for the grooms. My shoes were in a pile on the floor and my toiletries and makeup were spilling out of a carrier bag next to the bathroom.

If it had been an option, I might have gone to bed, so it was probably a good thing my clothes were strewn across it. Instead, I was sitting on the couch with my legs tucked under me. Mindy had helped me get undressed and brought me a robe from the bathroom before sitting me down with a glass of neat brandy from the bar downstairs.

The brandy was warming my insides at least.

The killer had met his end, that was how people saw Samuel's death and maybe they were right. I learned that Harold had been found by Boris's group in a spare room. He was working, plugged into the internet with no interest in what might be going on elsewhere in the house.

Apparently, he was shocked but pragmatic about Emma's death – they had already split up and he was planning to leave as soon as the storm passed.

The wedding guests, now feeling safe, retired to their rooms. The storm still raged outside, the police still couldn't get to us, and we still could not escape. They could have chosen to continue partying in the ballroom, but the general mood was not one that supported anyone celebrating or being merry.

The house was quiet, save for the howling wind and rumbling thunder.

A knock on my door, brought me out of my near-catatonic state. Buster barked, as was his habit, and he levered his ample rump off the carpet to rush at the door.

'It's Vince,' he announced.

A second later, from behind the door, Vince called out, 'It's Vince.'

I didn't want visitors, but I wasn't rude enough to turn him away. 'Come in.'

The door opened, Vince poking his head through the gap and manoeuvring around my daft Bulldog as he wagged his back end and got in the way.

Vince closed the door again and stayed on that side of the room.

'I just wanted to check on you, Felicity.' He was using an earnest tone, letting me believe that for once his intentions were genuine and honourable. 'If it makes you feel safer, I will stay here tonight.' He saw me react and brought his hands up to ward off my response. 'I'll sleep on the couch, I swear.'

I let my rising ire relax again. I'd thought he was trying to take advantage of me in a weak moment when I might want the comfort and security human contact would provide.

'Mindy is next door if I need her,' I assured him. 'And I have Devil Dog to sleep by my bed.'

'Devil Dog?' questioned Vince with a raised eyebrow.

I found myself chuckling. It was a surprise because I had wondered if I would ever laugh again. 'It's what he calls himself. Buster thinks he is a superhero.'

'*I am a dark avenger,*' Buster corrected me. '*More anti-villain than superhero. I'm what criminals see when they have nightmares.*'

Eyeing me curiously, Vince folded his arms and leaned back against the door to my room.

'Yes, what's with that?'

'The talking to my pets thing? You wouldn't believe me if I told you.'

'Try me,' he encouraged. 'I've witnessed it first hand.'

Vince had succeeded in taking my mind off Samuel. It was the first time in the last hour I had been able to do that. If that had been his intention, then he was more generous than I gave him credit for. More intuitive too.

The feeling of the young man dying in my arms returned like a knife to my heart and instead of giving Vince an answer, my face crumbled again, and fresh tears fell.

I didn't want to cry. I most especially didn't want to cry in front of Vince, but unable to stop myself as the emotions I was trying to keep in check forced their way out, I found myself floundering.

He moved silently, crossing the room without me sensing he had until he was kneeling on the carpet in front of me. I let him pull me into a hug but being given a shoulder to cry on was exactly the opposite thing I needed because the next thing I knew, I was sobbing.

I was trying to regain some control when there was a knock at the door and Mindy walked in without being invited.

'Auntie are you awake still?' she called out as she came through the door from the hallway and into my room. She was yawning at the same time, her mouth wide open with no hand to cover it and her eyes squished shut as a result.

Only when the yawn passed did she open her eyes again.

'Oh,' she said, taking in what she could see and misreading it completely. She began backing out of the room again. 'You need to learn to lock the door, Auntie,' she scolded.

I shoved Vince away.

'Mindy, he just came to check on me.'

'I don't need to know,' she called back, scurrying back out into the hallway again.

'Arrrgh!' I vented my frustration while behind me Vince chuckled again.

'You might as well just accept that we are an item, darling,' he joked. I say joked but he was probably being serious.

Ignoring him, I called after my niece, 'Mindy, what did you want?'

She popped her head around the doorframe. 'The blood on the banister.'

I blinked a couple of times, mentally questioning whether I had heard her right and then, when I decided I had, wondering what she was trying to tell me.

'What about it?' I asked.

'How did it get there?' asked Vince. I twisted to look his way and found he had taken off his jacket and was now sitting on my bed. 'Hmmm. This is quite comfy.'

My eye twitched.

Mindy came back into my room, walking around the foot of the bed to join me in staring at Vince. She was wearing sports gear again though her feet were bare. Her shoulder length blonde hair, dyed pink, was pulled back into a loose ponytail and she was free of makeup – not that she needed it at nineteen.

'That's right,' she agreed with the pirate on my bed.

'What's right?' I begged to know, twitching my gaze from one to the other to see who would answer me first.

Vince reclined so his head was on my pillow, kicked his shoes off, and pulled his feet onto my bed. Before I could growl at him, he started to explain.

'Ian Riggs found blood on the banister. That's how we found out about Geoffrey being attacked, right?'

'Okay,' I agreed, not seeing the point he was trying to make. 'So?'

'How did it get there?' asked Mindy. Clearly, she had been giving this some thought. 'Geoffrey was attacked in the library. That's only a few yards away, but he fell to the floor unconscious and claimed he didn't see his attacker. He was only just regaining consciousness when we arrived. So how did the blood get to be on the banister?'

'The killer left it there,' I suggested.

Vince gave a shake of his head. 'Unlikely. Geoffrey was struck with a blunt instrument. Any blood would have been on that.'

'It was a lot of blood too, Auntie,' added Mindy.

'And it was fresh,' I murmured, recalling the image of Ian Riggs holding up his hands to show the fresh red blood on them.

Mindy grasped what I was saying. 'We were wondering about an accomplice earlier. Samuel was with us right before we found out about Geoffrey being attacked. I thought maybe Geoffrey had been lying in the library for a while but the fresh blood disputes that.'

Vince said, 'It means Samuel couldn't be Geoffrey's attacker.' He closed his eyes. 'It's not the only incongruity.'

Beginning to feel bewildered, I was about to ask what else he thought he knew when Buster started speaking.

'*I've been thinking about the scents on the bodies,*' he told me with a thoughtful tone. '*I started out wondering why I couldn't smell Samuel on Quentin when I first got to sniff him. If you remember, I could smell the scents of the men in the room because they helped to lower him to the floor.*'

I heard Vince draw a breath to start speaking and shushed him.

He lifted his head slightly and cracked one eye open.

'Buster is telling me about what he could smell.'

My statement was enough to get Vince sitting up again. 'He's talking to you now?' the private investigator wanted to know.

I nodded, listening to Buster, and not really paying attention to Vince. 'What are you telling me, Buster?' I encouraged.

Buster licked his nose, his big tongue rolling over it with a snuffly snort. '*Well, I know why I couldn't smell Samuel. The point is I could smell him, but he didn't smell like himself.*' I relayed my dog's confusing words to Mindy and Vince. '*He was wearing another man's clothes, so he smelled more like him and left a mixed scent behind.*' I saw what he was getting at suddenly. '*Then, when they found the clothes outside, they were so wet, I couldn't smell Samuel on them to be able to work out who they belonged to.*'

Buster was trying to be helpful. More than that, I realised, he was chipping in to try to solve a puzzle. Knocked sideways by grief, I hadn't given the investigation any thought in the last hour. It had been neat: Samuel killed three people and then got killed himself as the people trapped in the house with a homicidal maniac armed themselves and attempted to make sure everyone was safe. His death was a terrible tragedy, but not one many would shed tears over. The police would arrive to find the crime solved and the killer unable to argue with the accusations.

I explained to Mindy and Vince about the wet clothes having no scent, then asked, 'What else, Buster?'

Buster tilted his head to one side, ducking his left ear and lifting a leg to scratch it. When he finished, he said, *'Well, I think the killer has to be one of the people I could smell on Quentin, but that doesn't have to mean it was Samuel. His scent wasn't on Geoffrey at all. And it wasn't on Emma.'*

'What about Kevin?' I enquired.

Buster looked up at me. *'That's where it gets tricky. One was wearing the other one's clothes. Their scents were mixed, and it didn't occur to me I might be smelling two people intertwined as it were.'*

I wasn't sure what to be most impressed about. My dog's ability to articulate his thoughts in such a cogent manner, or that he not only knew the word intertwined but was able to employ it correctly in a sentence.

'But we know he came to the island without a reason to be here and that he has a connection to Quentin.' I argued. When I explained what Buster said, Vince sniffed in a deep and thoughtful breath.

'I've been working on this with Hopster and Graham for the last hour. They are still going through Quentin's files, but so far there's nothing more in the data and images they've recovered to show us why Samuel might have wanted to target Quentin.'

Mindy piped up, 'There's still the small matter that someone had to bring him to the island. We never did get to the bottom of that.'

'No,' I agreed, frowning. 'Our discussion got derailed, didn't it?'

Thinking on my feet and pacing to my wardrobe, I said, 'Ellis still has the list of cars. I need to see it. There is something very screwy going on. Quentin wasn't tied up, and I know we discussed that earlier and you said he could have been subdued somehow, but if Buster says Samuel's scent wasn't on two of the bodies, then we have a second killer. We already think Samuel had an accomplice …'

'It would explain how he got to the island,' Vince agreed.

Mindy was staring into the middle distance, her eyes focused on the inside of her head when she murmured, 'Or maybe the second killer used our belief that we had a killer here to cover up their own murderous intentions.'

The room was silent for several seconds as we all looked at each other. No one said a word as we all spun Mindy's idea in our heads.

It had horrible connotations.

Buster licked his nose and got onto all four paws. *'Is it Devil Dog time?'*

'Yes,' I replied, reaching into my wardrobe for something to wear. 'I dare say it is.'

Massive Incongruity

I made Vince wait outside and locked my door, checking to make sure it was secure before I undid the belt on my robe. Then I remembered his ability to circumvent locks and propped a chair under the door handle for good measure.

Much like Mindy, for once, I wanted to choose an outfit for my ability to move in it. Unfortunately, I had packed for a weekend at a wedding and had nothing but fitted dresses, elegant jackets, and matching hats.

The only footwear I had without a heel were my slippers. They were not fit for the task, so I accepted defeat and paired my Christian Louboutin black slingbacks with a black dress by Elizabeth Roman, a London designer I favoured. It was sleeveless, so I employed a black jacket as well.

All in black, just like a ninja, I thought as I checked myself in the mirror. The outfit really needed a wide-brimmed hat to tie it all together and perhaps a diamante clutch in a shocking colour clash to draw the eye, but I wasn't parading for people to see, I was trying to catch a killer.

Mindy was ready first, naturally, because all she needed to do was put her bra and knickers on under her sports clothes.

I had dressed in a hurry though, spurred on by my desire to find answers. Mindy, Buster, and I found Vince waiting outside. He was leaning against the wall and humming to himself. There was no need for conversation, not yet. That would come later and be frenzied if we discovered there was something to the ideas running through our heads.

I wasn't sure where we would find Ellis Carter, the house manager. I assumed he had a room on the premises, but we were going to check the office he took us to first. I had no number for him, so if he wasn't there, I was going to find Boris and get to Ellis through his boss.

None of that proved necessary, because Ellis Carter was at his desk with his jacket and tie off, his sleeves rolled up, and a half-drunk glass of dark liquid in his hand.

He looked weary.

'Mrs Philips, Mr Slater,' he aimed a nod of acknowledgement at my niece. 'How may I be of help?' He looked surprised to see the three of us dressed and ready for action, but he made no comment even as his left eyebrow crept up his forehead.

'The list of cars,' said Vince, advancing into the room. 'Can we see it again, please?'

The surprise on Ellis's face increased. 'Um, yes, of course. I have it here somewhere.' He began moving things around on his desk until he remembered where it was and took a notebook from a shelf to his left. 'Is there a problem?'

Vince and I crowded him, all but snatching the notebook from his hand in our haste to find the list.

Mindy told him, 'Samuel Wilson didn't kill Emma Banks and he didn't attack Geoffrey Banks.'

Ellis's face wouldn't have reacted any more acutely if Buster had delivered Mindy's line.

He blurted, 'What!' as he stepped to his side, bumped his chair, jumped, almost tripped, and had to put his arms out to his sides to steady himself. His reaction was startling enough to make us all look at him and not the list in the notebook. Finally coming to rest, he looked down at his feet, checking he wasn't going to fall over, then looked back at our faces. 'What?' he repeated a little more calmly than before.

'There's a second killer on the island,' Buster growled in his rasping Devil Dog voice.

Here's a thing – I could convince Mindy and Vince to listen to me translating Buster's words, but I doubted a judge would be willing to put my Bulldog on the stand as an expert witness. I needed to explain how it was that we knew Samuel hadn't touched Emma and Geoffrey without telling people about my 'ability'.

'We are less than convinced Samuel was guilty of all three murders and the attack on Geoffrey. That means there is someone else involved and we need to work out who that could be.' I told him.

Vince had Ellis's notebook open on the desk with the list of cars displayed. Next to each was the name of the person who claimed to own it. The listing next to Vince's was still blank, Ellis not bothering to fill it in after he discovered the search was a dead end.

Mindy and Vince were both staring down at the notebook, leaning on the edge of the desk as they scrutinised the information.

Mindy had her lips pursed and a deep frown. 'I'm not seeing anything,' she huffed. 'All the cars have owners – which we already knew, but how do we work out which of them might have carried Samuel?'

Trying to approach the problem logically, I said, 'We can probably eliminate some of them. I had to peer around her arm until Vince noticed he was blocking my view and stepped back.

He agreed with me. 'Bruce Force arrived in a Ferrari. That model only has two seats, and his girlfriend was with him. The luggage space is too small for a man to fit in, especially one Samuel's size. We can cross them off the list.'

Mindy snatched up a handy pen and did just that, scribing a line across the page. There was another entry with a similar crazy sports car two people would fit in, but which left no room for Samuel.

That was it though. We had another two dozen cars to account for.

'Could he have come in the delivery van?' asked Mindy, spitballing an idea. 'Maybe the driver never knew he was there. He might have hopped in at a service station or something.'

Vince sucked some air between his teeth. 'It sounds too random. I'm not saying that couldn't happen, but it doesn't help us if he did because we can be certain the delivery driver wasn't complicit in his own murder.'

Staring down at the page and reading each entry for the twentieth time, my pulse hammered hard enough to make my eyesight spin when I spotted the answer.

I slumped and had to catch myself, both Vince and Mindy reacting with a startled jump as each thought they might have to grab me.

'Geoffrey!' I managed to blurt. 'It was Geoffrey!'

Ellis crowded in too, taking my place at the desk as I staggered away. The floor felt like it was moving beneath my feet. The groom had done it and now I had his name in my head I could not only see why but all the clues were beginning to line up.

'I'm not seeing it,' said Mindy, her eyes still glued to the page of the notebook.

Vince was just as dumbfounded. 'What makes you think it was Geoffrey Banks?' he prompted me to explain.

I slumped into Ellis's desk chair and let it roll back a foot.

'Look at the list of cars.' I left them with that instruction and tried to calm my heartrate as I thought about how sneaky he had been and how he ought to be starring in Hollywood blockbusters, not soap operas, given his obvious acting skill.

Vince spotted it first, a softly spoken expletive escaping his lips.

I saw him jab his finger and heard Mindy and Ellis repeat his unprintable phrase.

Ellis has written down the cars to form a list and then went around the guests to work out who each one belonged to. The guests claimed them, but it wasn't as if proof of ownership was required. On a list containing only high-end high-value marques such as Bentleys, Aston Martins, Ferraris and such, there were two vans. One was the caterer's, and the other belonged to the florist. There was one other incongruity on the list, a low-value Vauxhall Corsa, a lad's car. The type of car a young man like Samuel Wilson might drive. He hadn't claimed it though, Geoffrey had and not one of us believed it was actually his.

'So what do we do, Auntie?' my niece wanted to know.

'We have to confront him,' insisted Vince before I could form a sentence in my head.

'Surely, it can't be him though,' questioned Ellis. 'He was one of the victims.'

'The one who survived,' I pointed out.

Vince nodded along with my response. 'Ian Riggs said at the time he expected there to be more swelling at the wound site.'

'And that the cut looked too clean,' I reminded everyone. 'How better to throw off any suspicion than by being one of the victims? He made sure to lose everyone and cut himself. He probably hid the knife and threw the candlestick on the floor as an obvious weapon. He must have run along to the stairs to leave his blood on the bannister so someone would find him.'

'All he had to do was wait,' agreed Ellis.

Angry that I hadn't seen it earlier, I let my mouth ramble. 'He killed his ex-wife too. Maybe that's what this was all about. He brought Samuel here to help him – we questioned how Quentin hadn't fought back. I think they did it together. Maybe Quentin got in the way …' Something still didn't fit. I turned my attention to my dog. 'Buster, when we first went into the honeymoon suite, you said you could smell Emma.'

'That's right,' he rasped in his Devil Dog voice.

Ellis watched me talk to my dog and heard Buster's growl of reply. He then brought his eyes around to check that everyone else in the room just accepted the interaction.

'Is no one else concerned about Mrs Philips talking to her dog?' he asked.

Mindy shrugged at him. 'Not really.'

'Emma was in the honeymoon suite and it couldn't have been all that long before Quentin was murdered because Buster could still smell her when we got there.' I was frowning to myself, trying to figure out what that meant.

Mindy asked, 'You think Mr Banks killed his ex-wife because of their divorce? You said it was odd that she was on the guest list when they had such a public and messy settlement.'

I bit my lip. 'I don't know what I think.'

Vince had a go. 'We need to sit him down and ask him some tough questions but how's this for a theory: Geoffrey invites her here as a ruse to show the world they have moved on but plans to kill her. He knows Samuel somehow and either blackmails or otherwise coerces him into helping. Maybe the poor kid doesn't know what he is getting into, but either way, Quentin disrupts them when they are setting up the noose and they have to kill him, or he will know it was them. Emma must have been in the room just before that, but they couldn't go through with it because Quentin turned up. She must not have seen what was coming – maybe Samuel was hiding out of sight around the corner ….' I couldn't quite make it fit but believed quizzing Geoffrey with what we now knew would force him to fill in the blanks. 'Whatever,' I said dismissively of the holes in my theory. 'They kill him and before they can do anything about it, Anton comes out of the bathroom and discovers the body. After that, they are playing catch up.'

Mindy grasped the idea. 'Samuel tries to escape the island but finds himself cut off by the storm. He comes back to the house but by then we are searching for a killer and he has no reason for being on the island and he is soaking wet from being outside. He kills the delivery driver and takes his place.'

'That would explain the first two deaths quite neatly,' I agreed. 'What about the connection to Quentin? Samuel knows the first victim; we cannot ignore that.'

'Maybe it is just coincidence,' suggested Mindy.

I couldn't argue but I doubted it. 'Either way, I think we can assume Geoffrey lured Emma to the new honeymoon suite and killed her there before faking his own attack to cover his tracks.'

Mindy gasped. 'I've just remembered something!' We all looked at her. 'We all went running to find Geoffrey when Ian Riggs said there was blood on the banister. Well, Samuel was with us. He ran along next to me and he got to the library ... I remember him arriving because he stepped to the side to let me go in first.' She had a faraway look as she dredged her memory. Then she shook her head and focused her eyes back on mine. 'I don't remember seeing him after that. I think he came to the library, saw Geoffrey and decided to split.'

I drew in a thoughtful, yet worried, breath through my nose. 'It was right after that when Anton started talking about scouring the house to find the killer. The attack on Geoffrey followed by finding Emma dead in their suite were the last straws.'

Silence fell as each of us ran the terrible scenario through our heads. Geoffrey Banks, on the island for his wedding had chosen to lure his ex-wife here to kill her. Whether it was revenge for the divorce – she got the better half of their accumulated wealth – or something else that motivated him made no difference. He roped in an accomplice who should have vanished from the island long before anyone even knew he was here. Quentin bumbling into the honeymoon suite while they were setting up the noose and everything that followed were due to the storm and Samuel's continued presence on the island. Had Geoffrey asked Anton to search the house and kill his attacker? Had the groom whispered in Anton's ear until he found a shotgun and got trigger happy?

Vince sat back onto the edge of the desk.

'That's a heck of a theory. It's got holes in it, but it all makes sense.' Vince summed up our thoughts neatly. 'We only have one way of finding out if we are right. We have to confront him. Given that we know he has killed two people and been the cause of death for two more, this cannot wait until the morning.'

'Why not?' yawned Ellis. 'Everyone had gone to bed already. The storm is bound to blow itself out in a few more hours. The causeway will be exposed again shortly if the tide drops. Can't this wait until the police get here?'

I looked at Vince. 'He can't kill anyone else, not now that everyone thinks it was Samuel. He must think he has gotten away with it.'

Vince started for the door. 'That is as may be, but I will not sleep tonight until I know he is secured somewhere. There is no need to come with me,' he paused at the door to meet my gaze, 'This is what I do, after all, darling.'

It was one of those killer lines intended, I felt certain – to melt my will and make me go weak at the knees. Since I saw it for what it was, it had the opposite effect and my resolve to be the one who served the killer to the police on a platter returned.

I shoved by him, leaving the room first. 'Come along, Mindy. You too, Buster. We have a killer to catch. Follow us if you wish, Mr Slater, though I can assure you your debatable skills are not required.'

I heard his chuckle in the hallway behind me as I set my jaw and started back through the house to find my grooms.

I got two paces before the house was suddenly plunged into darkness. Involuntarily, I let out a squeak of shock.

Ellis swore. 'That will be lightning hitting the house. It will have knocked out the master breaker.' He tutted, annoyed at the extra work. 'I'll have to reset it.'

'Will that take long?' I asked, wondering if it might be better to wait until the lights were back on before we confronted Geoffrey.

He sighed and blew out a tired breath as he grabbed a heavy coat from inside his office.

'The master breakers are easy to get to, but it might have tripped at the junction box where power comes in from the mainland. That's at a junction box close to the jetty. Chances are, I'll have to go outside to get the power back on.'

Waiting was the sensible option, but that wasn't what I chose to do.

Shameful Guilt

The dark house with its sparsely lit hallways was an eerie place. I couldn't imagine wanting to live here tucked away on this island the way Boris did. All things considered I was glad it was one of the grooms behind it. In the morning, once the police were done with us, I would escape to the mainland and drive in a fast and very straight line back to my house where I would lock the door and spend many hours not thinking about the events of this weekend.

Oddly, as I made my way through Raven's Bluff toward what in theory was still my room even though I had given it up to the grooms, my thoughts returned to the royal wedding. Of course, until there was an official announcement, there was no royal wedding to consider, and even when such an announcement came, there was no guarantee it would be handled by anyone other than the palace despite rumours to that effect.

I wanted it. I wanted it badly. So bad I could taste it sometimes, yet I had to wonder what chance I stood now. The papers would get hold of the debacle and be all over it. A celebrity murder on a remote island with multiple victims? My name might not get printed at the start, but after the sham of Sashatastic's wedding two weeks ago where yet more people met their end, how likely was it that no one would notice the connection?

Primrose Green, my main competitor, would likely call all the papers and point it out to them.

A sigh slipped from my lips as I accepted that the chance to plan a royal wedding was most likely a pipe dream now. In some ways, I knew I ought to be glad that the pressure to stay in the race and all the stress such an event would cause were best avoided. I told myself to be happy I was going to find myself selected out of the running, but I couldn't quite get on board with the message.

I was still locked in my musing when a figure stepped out of a hallway that crossed ours to startle me with their unexpected presence.

'Anton!' I gasped.

He had dressed casually in jeans and a sweater, his outfit from earlier soaked from going outside on the roof. The groom looked just as surprised as me and had a hand to his heart and a grin on his face as he laughed his shock away.

'Goodness, you gave me quite a scare,' he chuckled.

'Where are you going?' enquired Vince rudely and in a tone that dripped with accusation.

Before Anton could snap out a response I interrupted. 'Anton, I need to talk to you. It's about Geoffrey. Where is he?'

The TV presenter swung a confused glance from me to Vince and then back to me.

'Why are you asking?' he wanted to know.

My stomach clenched – I really hadn't thought this through. When I left Ellis's office with Mindy and Vince in my wake, I was like John Wayne and was going to kick the door to the grooms' suite off its hinges. Now facing the man who's intended was guilty of triple homicide, I didn't know what to say.

I reached out to touch his arm, my voice soft. 'Anton ... I'

He flinched away. 'What about Geoffrey?' he demanded, his tone more forceful now. His face was flitting between mine and Vince's and I could see he suspected something. 'Was it him?' he gasped quietly, his voice nothing more than a gossamer whisper so close to silent I wouldn't have known he had spoken at all had I not seen his lips move.

I guess he could tell from our expressions that he was right because he fainted.

One moment he was looking right at me, the next his eyes rolled into the back of his head and he collapsed into a heap on the carpet.

None of us could move fast enough to stop him so it was fortunate that he didn't hit his head.

Buster ambled over to give him the kiss of life.

'Oh, no you don't,' I grabbed Buster's hips and held him back as Mindy darted in.

Anton came around again almost immediately, gasping as if shocked when the truth of his situation dawned on him again.

'Oh, Geoffrey! What have you done?'

I didn't want to answer – much of what we thought we knew was speculation, but I did say, 'It looks as though he invited Emma here just to kill her. The rest of it ... Samuel's involvement ... I think we need to ask him.'

Anton jerked spasmodically, twitching backward to get distance between us.

'I can't be part of that!' he cried.

Vince came forward. 'You suspected him though, didn't you? Why didn't you say anything?' He was looming and had a threatening menace to his jaw. Vince is a not a small man, and I have seen his displays of physical ability on more than one occasion. It was no surprise when Anton backed away another pace.

'I …' Anton looked panicked. His eyes were wide and filled with fear. In the next moment, his expression shifted to one of shame. 'I'm sorry. It was something he said a while ago. It hadn't occurred to me until then that he might want to harm Emma. Or anyone else,' he added as an afterthought. 'He was talking about acting and about how he had needed to act his way through this weekend with his bitch of a wife here. He hated her, you know? I was so surprised when he argued to invite her. He said it was all about public perception. He is a media sweetheart, but the tide of feeling swept toward her when he announced his true sexuality. She became the victim. It's why he caved to all her demands in the end, she made sure he was demonised in the press. I think he believed that if he could get through this weekend and publish photographs of her standing next to him and me at the ceremony, it would … well, set him back on the right path.'

'Does he own a Vauxhall Corsa?' I asked bluntly.

Anton frowned deeply. 'No. Why would you ask that?'

It was all the confirmation we needed.

Vince explained, 'Because when Ellis checked off the cars outside, Geoffrey put his name down against it. We think it is the car Samuel came here in.'

'How does Geoffrey even know him?' Anton questioned, clearly mystified by his lover's actions.

'That is what I intend to find out,' I replied, a little steel returning to my voice now that I felt more certain we had the right man.

Vince repeated his question from earlier. 'Where were you going, Anton? Your husband-to-be who, by your own admission, you suspect to be guilty of murder, lies with a headwound in Felicity's suite. The headwound is almost certainly self-inflicted, by the way, but you are wandering the halls. Where is it that you need to be?'

Anton hung his head once again, the guilty look returning.

'I was going to the car. Geoffrey asked me to get him a snack, and I was using the excuse to check on something.'

'What?' pressed Vince, though he wasn't the only one keen to hear what Anton felt a need to check.

Anton took a second to answer, sounding ever more convinced his intended was a killer when he said, 'The call log on his car. His actual car I mean. He has an Audi R8. That's what we came here in. I wanted to see if he might have called this Samuel chap from the car.'

Vince took a step backward down the hallway, moving in the direction of the stairs and the direction of the cars.

'I'll come with you,' he insisted, leaving no room in his voice for there to be a conversation about the matter.

I raised my eyebrows, shooting him a question as he began to back away with Anton starting to follow.

'We will not be long,' he promised. 'Don't go doing anything silly like confronting Geoffrey Banks before I get back.'

He turned to face the direction of travel and thus missed the deep frown that crossed my face.

As he vanished from sight around a corner and started down the stairs, Mindy came to stand next to me.

'I quite like him, Auntie, but your boyfriend can be a bit of a ….' the teenager searched for a word I might find acceptable.

'Yes, Mindy,' I agreed, cutting her off before she came up with a word for him. I had many of my own. 'Chauvinist? Misogynist? Pig? And, by the way, and not for the first time, he is not my boyfriend. Nor shall he ever be.'

'If you say so, Auntie,' replied Mindy in a tone that made it abundantly clear she didn't believe me.

Vince was a chauvinist. He expected me to wait for him because he was the man and confronting Geoffrey might be dangerous. He thought of it as man's work. To be fair, there was a voice inside my head that wholeheartedly agreed with him. However, I knew my niece's thoughts on the subject, and I knew how capable she was if Geoffrey, in his injured state, decided to resort to violence.

Scrunching up my face in a determined grimace, I swivelled around to face the right way again, and set off to speak to Geoffrey.

'Come along, Mindy. It's time we did what we set out to do. Let's solve this thing.'

She punched the air. 'Heck Yeah!'

Confronting a Killer

At the door to what was now the grooms' third honeymoon suite in less than twenty-four hours – I hadn't had a chance to move my things out yet or help to retrieve theirs – I simply opened the door and walked in.

I had never done anything so rude in my life and certainly not to one of my clients.

'Is that you, Anton?' called Geoffrey. The door opened into the bedroom, a large fourposter bed dominating the far wall. The covers were mussed, but not in a way that might suggest bedroom activity. It looked more like someone – probably Geoffrey – had been lying on top of the covers.

'Oh, wow,' Mindy exclaimed as Geoffrey wandered through from the bathroom with nothing on but a pair of slippers.

He choked and ducked back through the doorway and out of sight.

He sounded angry when he asked. 'What's going on, Mrs Philips? Did you forget you gave us your suite?'

He was going to demand an answer and attempt to kick us out. I cut him off before he could.

'Who is Samuel Wilson?' I demanded to know, levelling the question in a way that sounded like an accusation.

He was drawing breath to say something else when he realised what I'd said. It shut him up instantly – another nail in the coffin of his guilt.

Mindy moved to my left, getting some space between us I noticed. Glancing at her, I saw one hand reach to the small of her back where it rested, doing nothing.

For now.

Buster lifted his nose and sniffed. Snorting noises filled the air. '*Cat*,' he muttered. '*Lots of cat. They've been in here recently and Amber was with them.*'

'*Amber?*' I hissed from the corner of my mouth.

There was no time for a discussion about my missing cat though because Geoffrey had returned to stand in the doorway of his bathroom. He had a towelling robe covering his body, and the bandages still covering most of his skull.

They were not the things one would notice though. Anyone looking at daytime soap star Geoffrey Banks at this precise moment would want to know why his face was devoid of colour and why he looked so desperately scared.

'How do you know that name?' he begged me, his voice trembling.

I tilted my head to one side as I eyed him. He was guilty of killing three people and he was one heck of an actor because listening to his voice, I wanted to believe that he genuinely had no idea how I might know the name of his accomplice.

I told him, 'It's too late, Geoffrey. Anton knows.'

Geoffrey gasped, and fell to his knees, his shoulders shaking as he started to sob.

I had no idea what to expect. I'd only accused one person of being a murderer before and I'd got it completely wrong on that occasion. Whatever I might have imagined would happen with Geoffrey, this wasn't it.

'It was just a silly mistake,' he wailed.

Mindy hooked an eyebrow, her face questioning what we were seeing.

'I was flattered. He is so handsome, and sooo muscular. I couldn't resist him.'

'Wait,' Mindy's face showed the confusion I felt. 'Samuel was gay?' she asked, certain that was what we were hearing but needing to question it, nevertheless.

Geoffrey's bowed head lifted for a second. 'Of course. That's what this is about, isn't it? You just said Anton knows about my indiscretion. I've ruined everything.' He gasped and his eyes flared. 'Where is he?' Geoffrey jumped to his feet, bursting into action suddenly. 'Has he left? I have to get after him. I have to beg him for forgiveness!'

Shaking my head as if that might clear the fog of bewilderment now clouding it. I said, 'Samuel Wilson is dead. He was your accomplice.'

I don't think Geoffrey's reaction to my news could have been more extreme if I had inserted a cattle prod up his bottom. He clutched his heart, grabbing the bathroom doorframe for support.

'How? How can he be dead?' Before I could answer, the second part of my statement filtered through. 'What do you mean accomplice?'

I was getting bored with his act. 'Mr Banks you lured your wife here to kill her and brought Samuel Wilson here to help you with it. He was supposed to be gone before anyone noticed, wasn't he? He was going to help you to kill her and then escape, but the storm cut him off. At least we now know how the two of you are connected. Did Quentin stumble upon you erecting the noose?'

I was livid, my ire powering my voice as I put the pieces together and accused the groom of murder most foul.

'What on earth are you talking about?' Geoffrey cried.

'Oh, drop the act, you two-bit hack!' Rage filled my words. 'You killed a friend of mine because he was in the wrong place at the wrong time. He had a wife and children! Then Samuel killed the delivery driver when he got cut off. That's what happened, isn't it? Did you help? Was it you who strangled poor Kevin?'

Geoffrey backed away a pace. He had nowhere to go but both Mindy and I were coming forward, driving him back along the side of his bed.

Buster appeared from under the bed to cut him off from behind.

'*Stop right there, miscreant!*' he barked, shocking Geoffrey whose right hand was yet to leave his chest. '*Can I bite him now?*'

I didn't answer Buster, I was too busy revealing all that I knew. 'Did you really think that cut to your head would fool me? This isn't my first murder investigation, Geoffrey. You murdered Emma and ran to the library, pausing only to leave some blood on the banister so someone would know to look for another victim. Then what? Did you convince Anton to go after Samuel?'

'What?' he stuttered. 'You're saying Samuel was here? Why would he be here?'

Ignoring his question, I shook my head slightly to get a loose hair out of my face and sucked in a calming breath. It allowed me the second I needed to gather my thoughts.

'Do you know how we caught you?' I asked him. I expected him to say something to the effect that he had no idea what I was talking about. It was a recurring theme, but he just tracked me with his eyes as I paced to my right and looked at him with my head turned his way. 'It was the car.'

'The car?' he echoed, maintaining his act.

'The one you claimed was yours when Ellis Carter came around to check who owned which of the vehicles parked outside. You claimed a Vauxhall Corsa, but it's not yours, is it? It's Samuel's.'

I swung around to glare at the murderer, confident he was going to cave, but what he said gave me pause.

'I wasn't there when Mr Carter asked about the cars. I was on the phone to my agent to let him know about Mr Falstaff's death. I thought it might overshadow the press doing a piece about my wedding.' He had a curious look to his face now. It made me think something had just occurred to him and he was trying to work out what it meant. Also murmuring, he said to himself, 'Anton told Mr Carter what car we came in.'

I frowned, ready to argue with Geoffrey because his claim directly countered Anton's when the door opened behind me.

Mindy and I both twisted at the waist to see who was coming in. We expected Vince.

I did not expect the first thing I saw to be the barrel of a shotgun.

The Big Reveal

I had enough time for my heart to stop beating before Anton stepped into the room. The shotgun was in his hands and there was no sign of Vince. His face bore a slightly manic sneer but while the shotgun was aimed at Mindy, his eyes were glued to Geoffrey's.

Anton looked unhappy when he told his husband-to-be, 'It was a birthday present, sweetie. I knew how much you hated her. I knew how happy you would be if someone killed her, so I arranged for it to happen.'

My jaw fell open. So too Geoffrey's.

'You killed Emma?' Geoffrey could scarcely believe what he was hearing. I could believe it, but it threw every theory I had in the trash. If Anton was the killer, then I had no idea what was going on or who had done what and why.

Anton's face was a cruel grimace. Mindy's right arm moved slightly – I knew she had hold of the nunchucks tucked into her back. She was fast and she was looking for her chance to take out the man holding the deadly weapon.

Buster chose that moment to attack.

'*Dun, dun, DAH!*' he flew under the bed from the side, appearing at the foot to send the valance flying up like the hem of a skirt again.

I screamed, 'No!'

But I could do nothing to stop Anton squeezing the trigger.

Something in the back of my head took over, instructing my limbs to move. I dove forward, intending to get my body between the deadly blast from the shotgun and my stupid dog running toward it.

The boom and roar filled the room, hurting my ears and it came far too fast for my efforts to place me in danger. It was too fast for Buster too, whose lack of speed saved him for once.

Anton must have thought the dog would be moving faster because he blew a hole in the carpet a yard in front of my Bulldog who turned tail and ran away yelping.

The shot hadn't travelled far enough to disperse so the damage was limited to a circle roughly a foot across. It left another shot in the gun though.

Mindy was moving, her right hand whipping out and around with the nunchucks in it. Her grip was shifting so the weapon would open – she needed only a second to change our situation.

She didn't get it.

Anton had accurately assessed the threat, so having twitched the muzzle of the shotgun to fire a wild blast at Buster, he was already reversing it to aim at Mindy's centre of mass. He held the weapon at his hip, confident it was enough to stall her without needing to expend his second shot.

Mindy knew she couldn't win. The distances involved were too great and his choice of weapon meant he didn't even need to aim.

'Toss it,' he growled, his eyes and weapon on Mindy.

Reluctantly, and without taking her eyes off her opponent, she cast her ninja tool into a corner of the room. The odds swung ever more in Anton's favour.

It had all happened in the blink of an eye and I was on the carpet now, right where Buster would have been. He was nowhere in sight, most likely cowering under the bed in terror.

I got back to my knees as Geoffrey recovered from his shock and started talking again.

'You killed Emma?' he wanted Anton to confirm it.

'Yes. She deserved to die,' It was an admission of guilt. It proved me completely wrong – I am a terrible sleuth, and getting a solution to the case now was of little help because I could not see a way out of our present situation.

'Where's Vince?' I asked.

Anton twitched his eyes in my direction. 'Dead.'

It was a single word that hit me in the gut like a sucker punch.

The crazy killer with the shotgun had nothing left to say to me, his attention was back on Geoffrey.

'I found out about Samuel, sweetie.' Geoffrey hung his head in shame. 'I don't blame you, darling. I want you to know that. I took it to be nothing more than one last fling before you committed to me. I was going to let it go but do you know how I found out?'

Geoffrey lifted his face, his eyes full of question.

'That idiot Quentin Falstaff called you.' Geoffrey's brow furrowed; this was news to him. 'It was a week ago. You were in the garden, so I answered it. He didn't know it was me and he ...' Anton chuckled to himself at the memory. 'He wanted to blackmail you. You turned up at his studio to collect Samuel. I suppose you had a date.'

A tear fell from Geoffrey's right eye. 'I'm so sorry. I never meant to hurt you.'

Anton ignored him. 'You were there but you probably didn't know whose studio it was. You would have been excited to pick up the young piece of hot fluff, no doubt.' Geoffrey looked horrified by his actions being exposed to the one man he was supposed to love. 'Quentin Falstaff saw you through the window. Saw you kissing. He called and he thought he was talking to you. I knew he was our photographer, so I agreed to pay him and arranged for him to come to the suite.'

'What about Samuel,' I asked, unable to stop myself.

Anton's eyes narrowed in anger. He wanted to have a heart to heart with his fiancé and there were two intruders in his room. He kept his eyes on Geoffrey when he said, 'He was easy to track down. He had hopes to make it as a fitness model and he had a girlfriend with no idea her lover is actually gay. He begged me to not expose him.'

'And he agreed to murder Quentin?' Mindy questioned.

Again Anton's eyes tightened as the anger he felt threatened to overwhelm him. Was it anger at Geoffrey's betrayal? At being forced to admit the truth? Would he shoot one of us and then try to club the other to death? He would surely see Mindy as the greater threat but if I could get him to turn his attention to me, Mindy was the one who would stand the better chance of overpowering him.

'He had no idea what I planned,' Anton admitted. 'He really had no choice though. It was going to be simple: kill the blackmailer and leave. Samuel Wilson would have been able to go back to his life and no one would ever know he was here.'

'Except the storm cut him off,' I spoke loudly and with confidence. I needed him to focus on me.

'Yes, it did,' Anton agreed. 'Killing the delivery driver was all him. I had nothing to do with it. I thought Samuel got out before the causeway closed until I saw him later in the ballroom. At least he had the good sense to make himself scarce whenever Geoffrey was around.'

'It was you who hit me over the head,' Geoffrey shook his head in disbelief.

'I was as gentle as I could be,' Anton smiled warmly at his partner.

He whacked him over the head tenderly – that explained the lack of swelling at least.

Geoffrey shook his head, unable to comprehend the truth of it all. 'You knew people might look my way because you told Ellis that Samuel's car was mine.'

Anton didn't know Geoffrey knew that bit, but he shook off his surprise quickly enough.

'It is all academic now. What's done is done. I wanted to give you a wedding present, sweetie. Well, I've given you two. Your cow of an ex-wife paid for her sins and I am granting you your indiscretion with Samuel as a final fling. Now we can tie the knot and be what we always promised each other we would be.'

Geoffrey reacted as if slapped. 'Get married? You must be nuts! You're a psychotic homicidal maniac. The only thing I'm doing now is calling the police.'

Far from getting his attention to shift onto me, it was all on Geoffrey now, but the effect was much the same.

Geoffrey was across the room on the far side from Anton, who still held the shotgun pointed at Mindy. If she tried to get to him or it, a squeeze on the trigger would cut her in half so she wasn't moving.

I could see she was poised though.

Anton was showing his teeth, grimacing at Geoffrey while keeping one eye on the teenage ninja to his left.

'You will do as I say, sweetie,' Anton growled. 'I told you nothing was going to ruin our wedding and I meant it. Everything I have done was to protect us.' He was getting emotional, Geoffrey's threat that their relationship might be over too much for him to contemplate. 'I had to kill Quentin Falstaff, or he would have exposed you and made us both look like fools. I had to kill Emma because I knew how deeply she hurt you, and I had to kill Samuel because the idiot was going to get caught by the police and give it all away. All we have to do now is dispose of these two and we can live happily ever after.'

I heard a humming noise. It was arriving in my head without going through my ears.

Geoffrey couldn't stop shaking his head. 'There's no way, Anton. No way you can cover this up.'

'Yes, sweetie. Yes, we can. If you love me, we can do anything.' Anton was imploring his lover and more and more the shotgun was moving away from Mindy.

The humming increased. I took my eyes from Anton and the shotgun for the first time in over a minute. Just long enough to spot Amber coming through the door behind him. She was humming a happy tune to herself. It was not one I recognised, but then again, I cannot claim to know any great cat composers.

Geoffrey shook his head again. 'No, Anton. I will not be a party to this.'

Amber came up behind the man holding the shotgun.

Mindy had seen her too as had Geoffrey who had one eyebrow hitched to the top of his head in question.

'Yes, you will!' snapped the crazy murderer. His feet twitched, the shotgun started to swing away from Mindy as it tracked toward Geoffrey, and Amber slotted herself between Anton's feet.

Now, I've had my own experience of tripping over the cat and have often wondered if it was a deliberate act on their part when they walk under your feet while you are struggling in with the shopping and cannot see them.

Now I know it is.

In a manner that could only be described as expert, she threaded her body between his feet. He felt something, looked down, and tried to take a step as the unexpected creature there made him jump. As if able to anticipate what he would do, she moved to exactly where he would need to move his foot. At that point, he stood no chance.

He was falling backward a second later and the shotgun swung upward.

Now pointing in a harmless direction, it was still deafening when it went off to blast a hole in the ceiling.

Plaster rained down, and through it, Mindy lunged. Devoid of weapons, she was still a capable martial artist. I saw her right arm draw back.

Anton was recovering his balance, but he was going to pop back up in time to get a fist to his face.

Chase in the Dark

'Dun, dun, DAH!'

'No!' My scream of horror had no effect on my streaking fat lump of a dog. He shot out from under the bed again like a baked potato with eyes and feet.

Amber had moved away to one side and was calmly licking a paw as was her habit when she wanted to look cool and collected. Buster had no doubt seen what she did and felt a need to have his share of the action – he couldn't possibly let the cat steal all the glory.

However, what he did was run straight into Mindy as she stepped in close to Anton. Her scything punch was lancing down toward his jaw when all of a sudden her legs were no longer beneath her.

She let out an un-ninjalike squeal of surprise as she flew into the air, out of control, off balance, and without hope of stopping Anton as he scrambled to get his feet moving and ran out the door.

Buster dug his paws in to stop his forward momentum but still collided with the wall next to the door with a resounding thud.

'Did I get him?' he asked. *'I hit something.'*

'Even by dog standards, you are useless,' sneered Amber, running out of the door after the killer.

I was running too, chasing Anton though I doubted I could catch him. As I passed Mindy, she flipped herself off the carpet and back onto her feet.

'Ow!' she sucked air through her teeth and muttered some expletives. 'Buster!'

'*Huh?*' said Buster.

Mindy was limping and unable to put her left foot down. She waved an arm at me. 'Go, Auntie! I'll try to follow.'

I ran from the honeymoon suite, ducking left as I exited into the hallway. Anton was already turning to go down the nearest set of stairs. He had the shotgun in his hand but if he had any ammunition left, I hadn't heard him reloading.

Amber was nowhere in sight but that had been true almost the whole time since we arrived. She had vanished again, but with the shadows all around me, she could be less than a yard away and I would never spot her.

I ran to the stairs before I stopped to question what on earth I was doing. I'm a wedding planner in my mid-fifties – I can't chase killers. What would I do if I caught up to him? Ask him to surrender, pretty please?

I stopped at the top of the stairs, staring down into the gloom below. The brave part of me wanted to charge onwards and the sensible part said if I charged slowly, I might never catch up to him but would look like I had tried.

A groan from below got me moving because my brain knew it was Vince's voice I heard. He wasn't dead at all!

I flew down the stairs two and three at a time. Terrified for what I might find and praying Vince wasn't so badly injured a second man would die in my arms tonight, I skidded to a halt when I saw a set of headlights zip by in the darkness outside.

I was on the landing halfway down looking out over the rugged landscape. The storm had lost some of its power, and I couldn't see the sea to know if it was still thrashing the waves around, but guessing the car going past was Anton attempting to escape, I could not for one moment imagine how he could make it across the causeway.

Ellis said low tide was coming, but would that make the causeway passable? Surely not.

A second groan spurred me onward, down the stairs to the darkened hallway below. I couldn't see Vince, but I found him when I tripped over his foot.

I pitched forward, throwing my arms out to save my face from kissing the floorboards, and wouldn't you know it?

I landed on top of Vince.

He groaned again, but suddenly, as I was trying to get up, there was a hand on each of my hips.

'This is much more like it,' he rumbled. 'I don't mind you going on top at all.'

'Arrrgh!' I voiced my displeasure as I levered myself off the floor.

'Hey, where are you going, darling?' Vince wanted to know, the usual playful tone back in his voice.

The lights chose that moment to spring back into life. I had to blink against the sudden glow of light, but when my eyes adjusted, I could see why Vince was on the floor. There was a pool of blood around his head and a broken vase a few feet away.

'I guess we were wrong about it being Geoffrey,' Vince chuckled and winced. 'Ooh. I really shouldn't do that.'

Mindy appeared on the stairs behind me. She was limping along with an arm around Geoffrey's shoulders. Buster was at her side, moving slowly because he doesn't do stairs very well.

'Anton?' asked Geoffrey, hope in his voice.

I was kneeling to inspect Vince's head. Much like Geoffrey suffered earlier, but with the accompanying swelling and a far more jagged cut. Content that his brains were not going to spill out and that the well-dressed pirate was going to live, I twisted around to look at the groom.

'I think he went outside.'

The sound of running footsteps made us all look in the direction they were coming from. Even Vince levered himself onto one elbow.

Ellis came into view a moment later.

'Someone just drove toward the causeway!' Then he spotted Geoffrey who we had assured him was the killer and his eyes showed his surprise. 'Um,' he wasn't sure what question to ask.

'It was Anton, not Geoffrey,' I told him, my voice quiet as I thought about how I was two for two in the accusing the wrong person stakes.

The sound of more people came from above. Their voices echoed along the hallways above and down into the stairwell, increasing in volume when someone opened a door.

First to appear was Hopster, his face flush with excitement as he searched for something in the gloom. When he spotted Vince and me, he started babbling.

'It was Anton!' he gushed. 'We just got into Quentin's emails. There is a whole chain of them with Quentin demanding money and Anton agreeing to pay. There's even one where Anton invites him to come to his room this afternoon.' Hopster paused, bringing the laptop up to his face so he could read the text rather than attempt to recite it.

Anton had timed Quentin's arrival, luring him into a trap. There was no ambiguity over his intention – he was going to murder Quentin, not pay him. All the evidence was there now, and it explained why Anton 'accidentally' threw his pint over the laptop that he undoubtedly told Samuel to dispose of.

Next to arrive was Nat Spanks. Her face appeared over the banister, looking down at the five of us gathered below.

'I heard a shotgun being fired,' she claimed.

Mopping Up

With most of the house awake and out of bed, we gathered in the ballroom once more. It wasn't everyone on the island – there were still a few, notably Bruce Force and his girlfriend who hadn't even left their room for dinner. They were still locked away safely elsewhere, but most of the wedding guests were assembled yet again.

The sound of the shotgun had woken some, and the sound of those moving around and talking had woken others. I couldn't have slept if I'd tried; I was simply too wired.

Mindy's ankle was swollen, which I took to be a sign that it was just a sprain and not a break. It would heal itself in a week or so and in the meantime give my assistant a good reason not to wear heels.

Eric and Hattie appeared, or rather, they were spotted slinking by the ballroom. Ellis was escorting them from the island. When I got to speak to him later, he revealed that Boris had formally dismissed them both with immediate notice. Their personal belongings would be shipped to them when they provided an address. I almost felt sorry for them until I recalled how they behaved toward my grooms.

The police came a little more than two hours later. The storm was still going but it was peak low tide, if that is the right term, and the waves were no longer crashing over the causeway.

Three cars came plus a coroner's van. We hadn't updated them in a number of hours and DS Khan looked a little shocked that one coroner's van wasn't going to be enough.

'No one came over the causeway,' he assured us. We all knew what that meant. Anton was in the sea somewhere. A wave would have taken him and the car – we had already confirmed Geoffrey's R8 was missing. Would the car or his body ever be found?

Ellis Carter, the house manager, took DS Khan and a trio of other detectives to the rooms designated as honeymoon suites to show him Emma and Quentin, then down to the cellar to show him Kevin and Samuel. While they were gone, uniformed police moved among us, making sure everyone was okay and offering to make cups of tea.

The bar was free, no one took the tea.

Amber appeared again, sauntering into the room by herself. She made a beeline for me whereupon she jumped onto my lap.

'*You took your time working out who it was,*' she observed as she rubbed against me.

Buster, who was on the floor by my chair, got to his feet. '*Are you saying you worked it out ages ago, cat?*'

Amber peered over the side of my lap as I stroked her head. '*In truth, no. Not ages. I think it noteworthy that I worked it out first though.*'

I glanced around to see if anyone was paying me any attention, but they were not. Vince was dozing a few yards away, laid out on a couch. He had a head dressing not unlike Geoffrey's, which was no great surprise since Ian Riggs stepped in to apply his as well. Mindy was at the bar chatting to several celebrities. Her foot was bound with bandages, and she was getting sympathy and proving to be a hit with some of the younger men here for the weekend. Somehow, the nunchucks she set on the bar by her drink were not off-putting to the male suitors.

Satisfied that I could get away with it, I joined the conversation my pets were having.

'So how did you work out the killer's identity, Amber?' I spoke quietly though I doubted a casual observer would make anything of a woman talking to her cat. People did it all the time.

Mostly though, the cats don't talk back.

While I stroked her fur, Amber said, '*I told you earlier the cat in the room when the man was murdered said it could have been men and not a just one man. When you came back down the stairs from the roof, she spotted the man again. He was carrying a shotgun.*'

I could scarcely believe what I was hearing.

'You mean to say you knew Anton was the killer and you didn't think it pertinent to tell me!'

Amber began purring and paddling her paws up and down on my lap.

'*Now what fun would that be? Also, I was listening when he spoke earlier. He said Samuel was a model – How could he have known that if he didn't know Samuel?*'

I lifted my head, staring at the wall in disbelief that I could have missed such an obvious clue. I was a terrible sleuth and no doubt. That I had survived the day when so many lives had been taken was almost beyond belief.

The only thing I wanted now, was to escape Raven Island and never come back. Goodness knows what the reporters might make of it all. I just had to pray my name was kept out of the press. Otherwise, I could only guess what the ramifications might be for my business.

Epilogue: The Call

The following day, alone in my house with a large glass of expensive white wine (my second), I was peeling potatoes for my dinner when my phone rang.

It was not a number I recognised, so I answered it in my usual professional manner. After I recited my set piece, I waited to hear who might be calling me. Honestly, I was worried it might be the press. They had descended on Raven Island and were waiting for us when we started across the causeway to escape the house and all that had happened.

Someone, one of the tackier celebrities no doubt, had made a few calls. I didn't blame them, there had to be a scoop and some exposure to be had from the terrible events. However, I was relieved when the paparazzi peered into my car, failed to recognise me, and shifted their attention to the next car coming along behind mine.

The car behind mine was Mindy's. Photographers snapped a bunch of pictures, and she smiled gamely through her window until they realised she wasn't someone quasi-famous.

That was a little more than twenty-four hours ago now. I had arrived home feeling frazzled and on edge, but sleep, rest, a bath, and the peaceful quiet of my cottage in a countryside village, had combined to restore me to something close to my usual self.

Until the phone rang, that is. Now I found I was holding my breath, anticipating who might be at the other end of the line.

When, after a beat, a man spoke, I almost dropped my glass of wine.

'Mrs Philips, this is Edgar Whitechapel, I am valet to Prince Marcus, Duke of Canterbury.' My heart rate trebled, and my mouth went dry. 'Hello? Mrs Philips are you there?'

'Yes,' I mumbled. 'Yes, I am here. Good day to you, sir,' I replied when I found my voice. 'How might I be of service.'

'Very good,' his educated tones sounded in my ear. 'If you open your emails, Mrs Philips, you will find I have just sent you a non-disclosure agreement. I have a matter to discuss with you that must remain private.'

He was skirting around the subject but we both knew what it was. With my phone at my ear, I ran across the room to my laptop, hastily clicking the tab for my emails with fingers that insisted on shaking.

'I have it,' I let him know while trying to keep the tremor from my voice.

'Please sign it electronically where indicated and return it to me, Mrs Philips.'

'It's Felicity, please,' I told him as I did precisely as he requested – I wanted to be on first name terms with the man who was about to hand me my dream.

He came back with, 'Very good, Mrs Philips.' I guess we were going with formal then. There was silence for a moment before he let me know, 'I have it. Thank you, Mrs Philips. Now that task is complete, I can explain the reason for my call.'

This is it!

'Prince Marcus proposed to his long-term girlfriend, Nora Morley, last night. They are to be married at Canterbury Cathedral and not Westminster Abbey as one might expect as the prince wishes to honour his ties to the glorious county of Kent.' I swear I wasn't breathing while I listened to him speak. 'Part of his plan is to have all the firms engaged to cater and supply the wedding, the dress, the flowers, the carriage, et cetera, all supplied from within the county.'

'And you want me to be the wedding planner!' I blurted uncontrollably, my excitement gushing over in a torrent.

With calm dignity, Mr Whitechapel, valet to Prince Marcus, said, 'No, Mrs Philips, but the prince would like to hear your proposal for his wedding.'

'My proposal?' I was still trying to comprehend why he was calling me if he didn't want me to plan the wedding. I'd never been asked for a proposal before.

'Yes, Mrs Philips. Prince Marcus and his betrothed wish to meet with you to discuss your vision for their nuptials. You will need to present your estimated budget separately, though there is as yet no budget assigned for this event. You should include all elements of the wedding, from the formal banquet the night before to the ceremony itself and the wedding breakfast afterward. This will need to be presented as a business plan listing those firms you wish to employ and why.'

A question was pounding against the front of my skull demanding I let it out. 'How many other wedding planners have been asked to present their grand concept to the prince?'

I got a simple, yet elusive, answer, 'All those within the county of Kent with sufficient standing and portfolio to qualify them, Mrs Philips. Do you accept this invitation?'

My brain continued to spin as I mumbled, 'Yes. Thank you very much. This is such an honour. Please convey my good wishes and congratulations to the Prince and Nora Morley.'

Mr Whitechapel thought it necessary to give me a final warning about the non-disclosure agreement and what it would mean for me to leak the story before ending his call. There would be further instructions to follow in a subsequent email.

His words echoed in my head – all those wedding planners whose portfolio and standing qualified them. That meant at least two other firms, possibly three. I could name them all without needing to think. At the top of the pile was Primrose Green. She would be going out hard to get this, but I suspected she would be satisfied to lose provided she didn't lose to me.

I realised as I pondered my errant thought, that I felt exactly the same.

I drew in a deep breath and did my best to steady myself. This was the same competition I faced every day. I was the best in the business and my rivals knew it. I had the connections, the reputation, and the savvy to know my opposition were all quaking in their boots right now.

There would be no dirty tactics, not from me at least. I was going to score the royal wedding on merit. They would have to beat me – I am the competition.

So why was I feeling so utterly terrified?

The End

Author's Note

Unusually for me, it is not the dead of night as I finish this book, it is nearing dinner time on a Monday and the sun is shining outside of my log cabin. I smashed almost ten thousand words in a flurry today to finish a story which has been something of a trial to write.

Now that you are at the end of it, I hope you will agree that it was a convoluted web of intrigue and mystery with so many clues there isn't a reader on the planet who will solve it before they get to the end. That was what I intended, however, it got so convoluted, I struggled to keep it straight in my own head.

I like to write my books from start to finish as swiftly as I can. This works best for me because I stay in the story – a term I use to describe my headspace. The more time I spend writing, the easier it is to write. Unfortunately, this time around, a few minor inconveniences came along to disrupt me.

They are not noteworthy enough to mention here and too trivial to bore you with – we'll call them boring life dramas and leave them at that. Anyway, this particular book took nearly four weeks to finish which is two weeks longer than average and I am quite glad to have reached the end.

Raven Island does not exist. There are islands off the Kent coast but none so dramatically romantic and exciting as the one I describe here. The English Channel, that thin body of water separating England from Europe does not produce the kind of waves I write about either. Not often, anyway. We had a hurricane hit our coast in 1987, but that is the only one in living memory.

It is late spring now in my quiet corner of Kent. The garden is bursting into life and my five-year-old wants his paddling pool out every day. It's not quite warm enough for that, but as lockdown restrictions ease at the end of the Covid pandemic (fingers crossed), we do have a party planned for two weeks' time. Government guidelines allow it, so we will fill our garden with people. My wife has organised a bouncy castle and a soft play area and both our children will finally be able to have the birthday parties they missed.

For me, having a party is all about sharing the joy of making it through what has been a tough time for the country. Many have suffered, some are no longer with us, but for those of us who are left, I plan to take a moment to consider how lucky we are.

I might even relax and have a beer.

Until then, I have less than two weeks to finish the next book. Patricia and her friends are well overdue an outing so tomorrow I will be hard at it crafting *Dangerous Creatures*. I cannot wait.

Take care.

Steve Higgs

What's next for Felicity Philips?

Aisle Kill Him
Felicity Philips Investigates Book 8
Steve Higgs

Marriage. It can be absolute murder.

At a wedding fayre in a prestigious London hotel, Felicity Philips is in her element …

… until something terrible happens in her booth and all eyes swing her way.

Convinced arch-rival, Primrose Green, is behind it, Felicity knows she will have to find the proof before she points the finger. That might not be that easy though. She needs to schmooze the top clients perusing the companies on show – if she doesn't then Primrose will, and there's the small matter of the royal wedding to consider – reputation is everything.

Thankfully, she's got help. It comes in the form of her teenage, part-ninja niece, Mindy, vastly superior cat, Amber, and dumb but enthusiastic dog, Buster. Together, the foursome will have to pit their wits to catch Primrose in the act of dastardly sabotage.

But when a second terrible accident occurs, even Felicity begins to doubt her assumptions. Whoever is behind the events, they have more than mischief in mind and now that Felicity has poked her nose in, there is a target on her back.

Planning a wedding can be murder, let's hope it's not hers.

A FREE Rex and Albert Story

There is no catch. There is no cost. You won't even be asked for an email address. I have a FREE Rex and Albert short story for you to read simply because I think it is fun and you deserve a cherry on top. If you have not yet already indulged, please click the picture below and read the fun short story about Rex and Albert, a ring, and a Hellcat.

When a former police dog knows the cat is guilty, what must he do to prove his case to the human he lives with?

His human is missing a ring. The dog knows the cat is guilty. Is the cat smarter than the pair of them?

A home invader. A thief. A cat. Is that one being or three? The dog knows but can he make his human listen?

More Cozy Mystery by Steve Higgs

A desperate call for help is more than enough to get Patricia and friends in motion, especially when the call is from Patricia's socialite friend and zoo owner, the rather gin-soaked Lady Mary Bostihill Swank.

Her husband, George, an acclaimed thriller writer, has gone missing from her home but there is no ransom note and no sign of foul play. With no crime to investigate, the police are doing nothing and that's not good enough for Patricia.

Amid a backdrop of strange occurrences, which include jewellery stolen from inside Lady Mary's mansion, a note that suggests George might have been kidnapped by Bolivian freedom fighters, and a lady tiger somehow pregnant from immaculate conception, the team must wade through a confusion of clues to find the truth.

Will they be too late? Is George dead or alive? Will Lady Mary run out of gin?

With Patricia's ability to attract trouble working overtime, every hour counts, but as she begins to close the net, the dangerous creatures that surround them reveal a far more deadly crime is taking place ...

Solving mysteries can be murder.

Baking. It can get a guy killed.

When a retired detective superintendent chooses to take a culinary tour of the British Isles, he hopes to find tasty treats and delicious bakes ...

… what he finds is a clue to a crime in the ingredients for his pork pie.

His dog, Rex Harrison, an ex-police dog fired for having a bad attitude, cannot understand why the humans are struggling to solve the mystery. He can already smell the answer – it's right before their noses.

He'll pitch in to help his human and the shop owner's teenage daughter as the trio set out to save the shop from closure. Is the rival pork pie shop across the street to blame? Or is there something far more sinister going on?

One thing is for sure, what started out as a bit of fun, is getting deadlier by the hour, and they'd better work out what the dog knows soon, or it could be curtains for them all.

More Books by Steve Higgs

Blue Moon Investigations

Paranormal Nonsense

The Phantom of Barker Mill

Amanda Harper Paranormal Detective

The Klowns of Kent

Dead Pirates of Cawsand

In the Doodoo With Voodoo

The Witches of East Malling

Crop Circles, Cows and Crazy Aliens

Whispers in the Rigging

Bloodlust Blonde – a short story

Paws of the Yeti

Under a Blue Moon – A Paranormal Detective Origin Story

Night Work

Lord Hale's Monster

The Herne Bay Howlers

Undead Incorporated

The Ghoul of Christmas Past

Patricia Fisher Cruise Mysteries

The Missing Sapphire of Zangrabar

The Kidnapped Bride

The Director's Cut

The Couple in Cabin 2124

Doctor Death

Murder on the Dancefloor

Mission for the Maharaja

A Sleuth and her Dachshund in Athens

The Maltese Parrot

No Place Like Home

Patricia Fisher Mystery Adventures

What Sam Knew

Solstice Goat

Recipe for Murder

A Banshee and a Bookshop

Diamonds, Dinner Jackets, and Death

Frozen Vengeance

Mug Shot

The Godmother

Murder is an Artform

Wonderful Weddings and Deadly Divorces

Dangerous Creatures

Albert Smith Culinary Capers

Pork Pie Pandemonium

Bakewell Tart Bludgeoning

Stilton Slaughter

Bedfordshire Clanger Calamity

Death of a Yorkshire Pudding

Cumberland Sausage Shocker

Arbroath Smokie Slaying

Dundee Cake Dispatch

Lancashire Hotpot Peril

Felicity Philips Investigates

To Love and to Perish

Tying the Noose

Aisle Kill Him

Real of False Gods

Untethered magic
Unleashed Magic
Early Shift
Damaged but Powerful
Demon Bound
Familiar Territory
The Armour of God

Free Books and More

Get sneak peaks, exclusive giveaways, behind the scenes content, and more. Plus, you'll be notified of Fan Pricing events when they occur and get exclusive offers from other authors because all UF writers are automatically friends.

Not only that, but you'll receive an exclusive FREE story staring Otto and Zachary and two free stories from the author's Blue Moon Investigations series.

Yes, please! Sign me up for lots of FREE stuff and bargains!

Want to follow me and keep up with what I am doing?

Facebook